The

MANX MURDERS

The MANX MURDERS

A Professor Niccolo Benedetti

Mystery

•

WILLIAM L. DEANDREA

**OTTO
PENZLER
BOOKS**

NEW YORK

FICTION

Copyright © 1994 by William L. DeAndrea

Otto Penzler Books
129 West 56th Street
New York, NY 10019
(Editorial Offices only)

Macmillan Publishing Company
866 Third Avenue
New York, NY 10022

Maxwell Macmillan Canada, Inc.
1200 Eglinton Avenue East, Suite 200
Don Mills, Ontario M3C 3N1

Macmillan Publishing Company is part of the Maxwell Communication Group of Companies.

Library of Congress Cataloging-in-Publication Data
DeAndrea, William L.
    The Manx murders: a professor Niccolo Benedetti mystery / William L. DeAndrea.
    p.   cm.
    ISBN 1-883402-66-2
    1. Benedetti, Niccolo (Fictitious character)—Fiction.   2. College teachers—Fiction.   I. Title.
    [PS3554.E174M36   1994b]
    813'.54—dc20   93-47428

Otto Penzler Books are available at special discounts for bulk purchases for sales promotions, premiums, fund-raising, or educational use. For details, contact:

Special Sales Director
Macmillan Publishing Company
866 Third Avenue
New York, NY 10022

10   9   8   7   6   5   4   3   2   1

Printed in the United States of America

*Dedicated to the memory
of Robert D. Sampson,
whose love of the genre—
and his kindness to me—
lasted until the very end.*

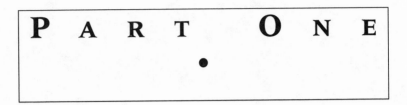

PART ONE

O n e

"Evil," the Professor said when it was all over, "is not a matter of sheer magnitude. It is a matter of intent, and of attitude. A man who teases a child because he likes to hear it cry may be more evil than a barbarian who slaughters thousands. It is an easy distinction to forget, *amico*. I myself have forgotten it for long periods of time."

"When, *Maestro*?"

"Too many times to recall. Most recently, with regard to the Pembroke brothers in Pennsylvania."

Ron Gentry knitted his brows and adjusted his spectacles. "When?"

"I have just told you."

"I mean, at what point?"

"It is important for us to say what we mean."

Still the teacher, Ron thought. Still "training" me. Not that Ron didn't admit that he (even now) still had a lot to learn. But Benedetti could get insufferably pedantic at times.

He didn't say any of this. Instead, he said, "Of course, *Maestro*. At what point in the investigation of the Pembroke case did you forget that evil is not a matter of sheer magnitude?"

Benedetti's smooth, brown, angular face opened up in a smile. "Very good, *amico*. But to answer your question, I forgot at the very beginning."

"I got to Harville the same day you did," Ron said. "I was with you every second. I didn't notice you neglecting anything."

"I said the *very* beginning. When I was first asked to look into the matter by Clyde Pembroke, and again when both brothers asked me to do so." Benedetti leaned back in his chair. "That, you see, was significant. The two of them hadn't been able to agree on anything since early adulthood; yet they agreed they needed help, and they agreed that they needed me.

"In my arrogance, however, I decided both times that they were simply a pair of petulant old men, and, further, that they had nothing to offer my work."

The Professor's work was nothing less than the study of the question of Human Evil. Though he had tracked murderers around the globe, with and without the help of Ron Gentry and Ron's wife, Janet Higgins, the old man always bridled when anyone described him as the "World's Greatest Detective."

"I am not a detective," he would invariably say, with more or less heat depending on how peevish he was feeling. "I am a philosopher."

"Little did I know, eh, *amico*? Have I not always taught you that humility is the proper frame of mind in which to seek the truth? Yet there I was, too filled with my glorious pursuit of serial killers and madmen to recognize some quiet, domestic evil when it was presented to me."

Ron had never seen the old man like this before. Perhaps he was now truly getting old. Or perhaps Benedetti's latest love affair had burned out. It was hard to tell.

"Don't let it bother you too much, *Maestro*," Ron said. "You got the killer, after all."

"If I'd intervened sooner, there might have been no killings at all. I should not have waited for dear Janet's friend to ask me on behalf of the government. I should not have waited for the disappearance of the birds . . ."

T w o

When the plane landed yet again, Ron Gentry got out and stretched his legs. The airport was on a rockbound coast, and that water out there was the North Atlantic. He was pretty sure he was in Maine by now. Oh, sure. He was. A fellow had poked his head into the plane two airports back and asked him if he'd had anything to declare.

He could have declared he'd never been more tired in his life, or that he liked flying, but only if the plane spent a minimum thirty minutes in the air before coming in for a landing. This one had not, not since he'd taken off from Nova Scotia that morning.

What had brought him to Nova Scotia was a case. An insurance case. Ron Gentry did a lot of those. When he wasn't trailing Benedetti around the world, usually in the middle of some high-profile case that had the attention of millions, Ron filled his time doing what every other private eye did— finding witnesses for lawyers, making sure insurance claimants really were disabled, things like that. No divorce work. Before he'd made that rule, Ron had learned that the average divorce (at least the ones that got to the stage of one party or another hiring a private eye) was messier and more depressing than the average ax murder.

This particular insurance case had almost turned into a missing-persons job. The person he was supposed to interview wasn't hiding from anybody; he just had wanderlust. Ron had tracked him all over the Northeast before catching up to him in a province of what was (for the moment) still Canada. Then he began puddle-jumping back home.

Here, in fact, he was supposed to change planes for one

that would take him west, back home to the city of Sparta in Central New York. Home to Janet. He missed her.

He knocked on the door of the plane, a six-seater. The pilot grinned at him. The man had white hair, and a close-clipped little mustache along his upper lip. Probably a souvenir of RCAF service in World War II. He looked old enough.

"Can I go inside?" Ron asked.

"Sure, go ahead. I just want to finish the flight reports." The pilot lifted a clipboard from his lap, held it up for Ron to see. "I'll bring your bag in pretty soon. There's plenty of time, you know."

"I know," said Ron. He had a ninety-minute layover coming up. That much he remembered. He wished he could remember where he was. "What I mean is, is it safe to walk across the concrete like this, or am I going to get chopped up by somebody's propeller?"

"We all try to avoid that, you know. Chopping things up with the propeller is bad for the plane. That's why they're—"

Ron grinned and nodded. He didn't exactly want to get into a conversation with the guy. It was late September, and it was gray and damp out here. You couldn't exactly call it foggy, but the humidity in the air and the salt mist from the ocean (he could hear waves splashing) combined to make a potion that seeped the cold right through him.

Also, he didn't want to stand out on the runway.

Ron made his way to the terminal. The terminal was an apple-green, aluminum-sided shacklike structure about forty-five yards away. If it weren't for all the antennae and the wind sock on the roof, it could have passed for a two-car garage in any semidepressed neighborhood anywhere in the country.

As he crossed the tarmac, he began to sniff. Not because he was catching cold (although he wouldn't have been surprised if he were), but because he smelled something. Soda. Candy. Something like that.

Probably his mind playing tricks. He thought he'd smelled it a time or two before, that day. He'd read somewhere that people often smelled sweet smells—melon was most usual—just before having a stroke.

Golly, he was just loaded with cheery thoughts today. At least this scent wasn't melon, he told himself. Was it? He sniffed again. No. Grape. Artificial grape, at that, like candy and soda.

Maybe I'm about to have an artificial stroke, he thought.

If he eluded the stroke, he was likely to keel over with fatigue. Candy or soda was a good idea, he decided, quickening his steps. The sugar rush would keep him from dozing off and missing his next flight. God knew how long he'd have to wait here if he did that.

He walked into the terminal. It was basically one room, with a little glassed-in place like a ticket booth built into one wall. A combination ticket booth and control tower. Or something. There were bus station plastic seats in depressingly gay pastels against the other walls, interspersed with vending machines.

The place was clean, Ron had to give it that much. There wasn't so much as a gum lump on the concrete floor. Ron was reaching into his pocket for change, confident he could eat a couple of Bar Nones and drink a Coke Classic in perfect hygienic safety.

He had the first quarter poised to go into the first slot when a voice said, "Misteh Gentry?"

Ron turned around to see the guy from the Pepperidge Farm commercials looking at him from behind the glass. Ron looked back over.

"I'm Gentry."

"Figured you must be. Got a message for you."

"For me?"

The guy said, "Ayuh," and Ron looked at him hard. When

anybody lived up to stereotype, Ron always suspected he was being put on. Still, a hard look revealed no signs of mockery. Ron decided there must really *be* people in Maine who said "Ayuh."

"Who knows I'm here?" Ron wondered aloud. "*I* didn't even know I would be here. I was going to call my wife and let her know."

"That's the message."

"I beg your pardon?"

"Call your wife. That's the message."

"That's all it says?"

The guy in the window consulted a piece of paper. "'Tell him to call his wife,'" he read. "That's all I've got."

"Okay, thanks. Where's the phone?"

"In the corner, there."

Ron saw it, said thanks again, and headed for it, wondering what was up. He'd been away on business before; he always checked in as soon as he could. He wondered why Janet had tracked him down through the pencil-kept records of some of America's tiniest airlines to tell him to do what she had good reason to suspect he was going to do anyway.

He hoped nothing was wrong.

He dialed, waited for the bong, heard the heartwarming tape thanking him for using that particular long-distance company, then finally the ringing, succeeded by Janet's low, soft greeting.

"Hello. I got here. I love you, I miss you. What's up?"

There was an odd hesitation.

"Janet?"

"Yes, darling. I love and miss you, too."

There was laughter in her voice. Ron felt instantly better.

"It's the Professor," Janet went on.

"What about him? Is he okay?"

"Oh, he's fine. At least he was when he left."

"When he left? Where did he go?"

"Harville, Pennsylvania. He wants you to meet him there as soon as possible."

"He must be out of his mind. He's been scorning the Pembroke brothers for months now."

"He changed his mind."

"Any inkling of why?"

"They brought out the heavy artillery."

"That leathery old hide is immune to artillery."

"They sent up Flo Ackerman."

"Flo Ackerman is the heavy artillery?"

"Flo Ackerman is an old friend of mine. My best friend from college. She's with the Environmental Protection Agency."

"If she's such an old friend, why wasn't she at our wedding?"

"She was in Poland at some kind of conference. She sent us a present."

"What?"

"The portable hot-air convection oven."

"Oh, that's where we got that. Did we thank her?"

"I was raised properly, Mr. Gentry. Our thank-you notes were mailed before we were done with our honeymoon."

"When did you have time?"

"Sometimes you took a shower by yourself."

Ron felt himself grinning. "That was foolish of me. Anyway, what kind of leverage does your old friend have on Benedetti, for crying out loud? And what does she have to do with the Pembrokes?"

"I can answer the second question. The Pembrokes have developed some kind of device that pulls smoke out of a smokestack magnetically, and collects it to be burned again. Or something. The EPA wants them to manufacture the device, but one of the brothers refuses, and the whole business is in an uproar. Apparently, on anything that involves build-ing on to the plant, the brothers have to agree, and they won't because they hate each other's guts."

"We knew that. So the Professor is off at the beck and call of his adopted country again?"

"It was more than that. He said something about the birds being gone. A sign of evil, all the birds are gone."

"Maybe the cats got them." When the Professor had first been approached about the Pembrokes' problems, Ron had done a little background check. Clyde Pembroke raised cats, champion Manx cats, the kind without tails.

"Ron," Janet said. "Be serious."

"Oh, all right, if I must. Now I have to figure out how to get to Harville, Pennsylvania, from here."

"I've got that all taken care of," she said.

"Actually, I figured you would have, but I didn't want to sound as if I were taking you for granted."

"That," Janet said, "is why our marriage is the envy of the world."

"Precisely," Ron said. He was very happy. When they'd first met, Janet had been too insecure to make that sort of joke. In the years they'd been together, she was learning to take him for granted, or at least to count on the way he felt about her, and that was exactly the way he wanted it.

"Get back on the plane you just got off," Janet instructed him. "That will take you to Springfield, Massachusetts. From there, you get a flight to White Plains, New York, and from there, you can get USAir flight nine-ninety-six to Scranton. There'll be a rental car at the airport for you. Everything's all arranged."

"Great. What do I do, meet you in Scranton?"

"No. You go to the Keystone Inn in Harville and meet the Professor."

"What time do I pick you up?"

"Not for a couple of days. I've got something I've got to take care of up here."

Ron bit his lip. It was childish, he knew, but he wanted to be with his wife, and now there was going to be further delay. He didn't want to nag her about it. Not nagging was another one of the things that made their marriage the envy of the civilized world.

"Okay," he said. "I'll miss you, though. Don't take too long, all right?" Ron heard himself, and wondered if he was nagging.

If he had been, Janet let it pass. "Soon as I can," she promised. "I love you."

"I love you, too."

"You'd better get moving."

"Guess so," he said. "I'll call you when I get there."

"Don't forget. Bye."

Ron said good-bye, and hung up the phone with reluctance. As far back as he could remember, he had wanted to be a policeman. Genetics, in the form of acute myopia, had gotten in the way of that, and Ron had decided on law. *That* plan had lasted no longer than his first encounter with Niccolo Benedetti, who had grabbed him in a hallway at Sparta University and proclaimed in a loud voice that he had the look; that he would become Benedetti's next assistant.

That had turned out even better than being a policeman. He'd never had to hand out a traffic ticket; he dealt with no department politics. He jumped straight into the heart of the most important cases the world had to offer, and he loved every minute of it. Even in his more mundane work, his day-to-day PI stuff, Ron was doing what he'd always wanted to do. He'd never faced a case with reluctance.

Until now.

Now, instead of flying home to the warm arms of the woman he loved, he was off to some forgotten (but not forgotten enough) mill town in northern Pennsylvania to help the World's Greatest Detective (excuse me—philosopher) wipe the noses of a couple of superannuated crybabies who couldn't figure out how to work out their fraternal differences. Ron had never been much of a stickler about his own dignity, but somehow he felt this was beneath the dignity of Professor Niccolo Benedetti, and that bothered him.

He waved to the Pepperidge Farmer and headed out of the terminal, bumping into his pilot in the doorway. He was carrying Ron's suitcase in his hand.

"About face," Ron said. "There's been a change in plan. I'm going on to Springfield with you."

"Oh, that's nice," the pilot said. "I've got to go to Springfield, anyway, hell or high water, and I'd like the company. Good idea to get going quickly, though. I want to beat the weather."

Ron said, "Mmm." He had already noticed that the sky was darker now, a kind of slate gray. The damp cold had an autumnal edge to it.

He was close enough to touch the plane before he remembered that he'd blown his chance to get anything to eat or drink.

With a frustrated sigh, Ron climbed in and fastened his seat belt. His empty stomach started complaining to him just as they got airborne.

"Am I crazy, or have I been smelling something at these airports?" he asked the pilot.

"Oh, that," the pilot said back over his shoulder. "We get used to it, and it's a lot better than what went on before."

"Oh. What went on—" Ron began, but just then a flash of lightning lit up the inside of the plane, and a peal of thunder seemed to toss it around the sky, and there was no more conversation on the rest of the trip.

T h r e e

Florence Ackerman took one last inventory in front of the mirror. Makeup in place; lipstick—not overdone; earrings secure; no dandruff on the shoulders of her charcoal-gray blazer. She fluffed the flounce of her silk blouse, finger-combed her newly blond hair, and left the room, ready to face the world.

It was something she did every day of her life, even on Saturdays and Sundays in August down in D.C., when Flo knew not only that she was going to be the only person anywhere near the office, but also that, car air-conditioning or not, she'd look like a drowned rat by the time she got to her office.

She did it because it was part of the ritual of success. She could at least *start off* looking her best. Besides, cultivating habits of quality could pay off. This whole Pembroke business was important to the Agency, to the environment (and therefore to the nation), and to her career. It was a marvelous opportunity. The only reason she was here in the first place was that all her superiors—any one of whom could ordinarily have swooped up an assignment like this—had their eyes on the election results. Those who weren't political appointees yet were trying to be, and they were all busy buttering up politicians.

That suited Florence fine. She hadn't quite reached that stage yet, but she'd get there. And if any of the butterers were successful, that would mean room for her to move up, too.

Of course, there was another reason all the higher-ups in her section had passed on this assignment, one that Flo was too honest with herself not to admit—at a time like this, nobody wanted his buttery fingerprints on a failure.

Neither did she, but, then, she didn't mean to fail. If it took the famous Professor Niccolo Benedetti to get those asinine Pembroke brothers out of their respective snits and put the unit into production, well, she had gambled that her friendship with Jan Higgins would let her be the one to get him there.

And it had worked! The old man was ensconced in this very hotel, two floors up, and she'd just heard from him that his assistant had arrived, and that the two men were ready to be briefed.

Flo looked at her bulging Coach portfolio and reflected ruefully that she had plenty to brief them on.

And she was curious about something on her own. She wanted to see this assistant, this Gentry character. She wanted to know what sort of husband her old friend had snagged.

Benedetti himself greeted her at the door. "Ah, Miss Ackerman. Do come in, dear lady." The old man's voice and manner were elegant; for one mad moment, Flo was afraid he was going to kiss her hand. Instead, he merely led her to a chair, then sat himself.

Benedetti looked exactly the same as the last time she had seen him, up in Jan's house in New York State. Huge, bulky body, like a loosely connected pile of logs draped with thick tweed; small, catlike head with the sloping forehead and slick black hair; shining black eyes; blue-and-white polka-dot bow tie. But there was a difference. Up until the end of her last meeting with him, until the time he'd agreed to come here, he had been bored, almost resentful. Now he was alive. There was something about this that intrigued him. Flo would have to pin it down and exploit it. She wanted him interested and working until he figured out whatever was going on around here.

"It's nice to see you again, Professor," she said. "I hope the suite is okay."

"The suite is excellent. There are even good, big windows for my painting." He gestured toward a covered easel against the wall. "It will be especially good if the sun ever manages to come out."

Flo tilted her head. "I don't know if you'll have much time for painting, Professor."

He smiled at her. "I always have time. It is my way of speaking with my subconscious. But you must not worry. I promise the taxpayers will get their money's worth."

It was Flo's turn to smile. "I am happy to say, Professor, that except for my own humble salary and expenses, this is not costing the taxpayers a cent. The Pembroke brothers are paying your fee—all of it—and all expenses for you and your staff."

"*Va bene.*" Benedetti nodded. "Excellent. They will be the more eager to cooperate, then."

"They have been all along. Willing to cooperate, I mean."

"Not with each other. People who are willing to cooperate with each other do not choose experts on human evil to mediate their disputes."

Flo had to admit he had a point. "In any case, Professor, I want to thank you for looking into this. I truly—"

Benedetti held up a hand. "No thanks are necessary, Miss Ackerman. If this were truly a favor, it would be to your friend and mine, Dr. Higgins. But, in fact, it is no favor at all. I have simply come to believe I can further my work by looking into this matter and so— But here is Ronald."

Another man emerged from the other room. He said, "Oh. Sorry. Professor, you should have told me. I was just letting Janet know that I'd managed to dodge all the lightning bolts. Hi. You must be Flo Ackerman. Janet told me to give you her love."

The phrase "or yours" streaked involuntarily across Flo's mind. My God, she thought, he's *gorgeous*. Over six feet tall, naturally blond (unlike, say, Flo), well built, face just rugged enough not to be pretty, with the glasses adding just the right touch of intellectualism.

She was shocked. Back in college, they had always been gawky, mousy Janet and pudgy, pimply Flo. They'd come together out of mutual outcast status. Not that there was anything *wrong* with them. Janet was a refugee from a childhood as a musical prodigy in the South; Flo had been Green when all the young people she'd grown up with were too busy being Jewish American Princesses to be interested in the environment. To them, the phrase "natural habitat" meant Bloomingdale's, or its Sparta University equivalent, Farnum's.

Flo and Janet managed to scrape up a few losers for dates, but mostly they had each other to talk to, which was just fine with them. Graduation came. Janet went on to postgraduate work, eventually getting a Ph.D. in psychology. Flo had ridden a wave of sheer competence or affirmative action, she didn't know which, to the staff of the EPA. They'd stayed in touch.

Now, after ten thousand dollars or so spent on dermatologists and ten thousand skyscrapers' worth of exercise on her stair-climber machine, Flo was no longer pimply or pudgy. Thanks to L'Oréal (and she did keep reminding herself she was worth it), she was a blonde. And as far as she knew, Janet was still as gawky and mousy as ever.

But look what little Janet got to take to bed every night.

Flo was shocked again, this time at her own reaction. How dare her old friend show her up like this? Who the hell did she think she was?

She made herself stop. This was unworthy. This was stupid. And it was moronic, and *profoundly* antifeminist, to judge herself or any other woman on the basis of the man in her life. Surely her consciousness was above that.

"Miss Ackerman?" Ron Gentry said.

"Excuse me? Oh. Sorry. I was gathering my thoughts for the briefing. And, please, call me Flo."

"I'd be pleased to, if you'll call me Ron."

"Ron it is," she said.

"And the Professor likes to be called 'Professor.'"

The old man scowled at him. "*Basta.*"

Ron grinned. "*Certo, Maestro.*"

Flo unzipped her portfolio. Oh, hell, she thought. The glasses are probably a façade, anyway. He's probably dumb as a post. And no good in bed, either.

• • •

She held up an aerial photograph, in color, of a wooded area. It looked like an old stereopticon slide. The shot showed two Victorian mansions, maybe, Ron judged from the apparent height of the photo, three-quarters of a mile apart. The houses were identical piles of brick, four stories high, with slate-and-copper roofs and a great deal of fancy filigree on the windows.

"Two of them," he said foolishly. For a second, he saw a smirk cross Florence Ackerman's face, then she went on.

"The one on the right is Alpha House; the one on the left is Omega House. Both were built by Humbert Pembroke in 1923 on the birth of his twin sons, Clyde and Henry. Clyde is the elder by ten minutes.

"As children, the two boys were inseparable, and that lasted well into adulthood. They played in the same backfield at Penn. I've got a picture if you want to see it."

"Please," the Professor said.

She handed it over. Benedetti looked at it and passed it to Ron. "Which one is which?" the old man asked.

"Clyde is number thirty-four; Henry is number forty-three."

"Thank you," the old man said. "But I doubt they will be wearing their uniforms when I meet them, eh? Is there another way to tell them apart?"

Flo Ackerman scowled. Was the old man mocking her? Benedetti had that effect on people. Finally, she decided he hadn't been, which was a good guess on her part. Ron knew that when Benedetti actually did want to insult somebody, the insultee was left in no doubt about it at all.

"Well," she said, "you're not likely to see both of them at the same time, but there is a way. Clyde Pembroke has a purple crescent-shaped mark on his left brow. A forceps mark."

"You know a lot about them," Ron said.

Flo nodded ruefully. "I've spent months trying to get those two to stop bickering. I've found out everything about them that I could. Too bad it hasn't worked."

"Obviously," Benedetti said, "they are no longer inseparable."

"No," Flo said. "They're not. Their father died in 1950, leaving Pembroke Manufacturing in equal shares to 'the boys,' as everybody calls them—forget they're both around seventy.

"At that, they did a good job of it. Seemed always to be one step ahead of the future, if you know what I mean. Great environmental record. Pembroke Manufacturing switched to making electronic components and stuff early on, so they've thrived while other companies in the Northeast went out of business. Clyde and Henry are worth about two hundred twenty million each, as far as anyone can tell.

"They fell out about 1952. Clyde took up with a local girl named Sophie Havelka. Wrong side of the tracks in the days when that still mattered."

"It is an unfortunate facet of human nature, Miss Ackerman, that people will always erect tracks between themselves and their neighbors. The desire for unearned superiority is one of the most irradicably pernicious ones we possess. But I am interrupting you. Please go on."

"It's a short story," Flo continued. "Clyde was in love with Sophie, then Henry was, too, then she married Henry. They had a son, who lives at Omega House. I'll fill you in on all that stuff later. Sophie died ten years ago."

Flo pushed her hair off her forehead with her fingertips. Janet frequently made the same gesture. Ron wondered who'd picked it up from whom.

"The brothers stopped being inseparable when Henry wound up with Sophie, but they still got along. The real trouble started about five years ago."

"When Clyde got into cats."

"Exactly. You see, Henry is a bird-watcher. Fanatical. Most of his share of the Pembroke estate is a nature preserve, and he's gone out of his way to make sure all the birds native to this area have what they need to live.

"He was absolutely furious when Clyde decided he was a cat person. Said the cats would slaughter the birds."

"But," Ron protested, "purebred cats in a cattery are not about to be let loose anywhere, let alone in a nature preserve."

"I agree with you. And Clyde says it's never happened and never could happen. But Henry just won't be convinced on the subject. Wait until you meet him."

"With bated breath," Ron lied.

"Henry swears bird fatalities have risen since the cats moved in." Flo Ackerman shook her head, as if she couldn't believe what she was saying herself.

"So about three years ago, Henry retaliated. With the ice cream."

"With the ice cream," Benedetti echoed.

"That's right. Henry set his son, Chip—actually, Humbert the second—up in the ice-cream business. Gourmet stuff. Small batches, limited distribution area, high price. Chip's Creamery Ice Cream. I don't know if it's available as far north as Sparta."

"A couple of places," Ron told her. "I hear it's pretty good. How is that a revenge on cats? Or rather on Clyde?"

"The ice cream plant is on the estate."

"In the middle of a nature preserve? How the hell did that happen?"

"You've got to understand the socioeconomic picture, Ron," Flo began. Ron's eyes usually glazed over at the sound of the word "socioeconomic," but he forced himself to stay tuned in.

"For one thing," Flo continued, "there's a lot of the estate that *isn't* nature preserve, and that's where the plant is. For another thing, there's virtually no unemployment in this town, while towns all around here are dying slow deaths. I don't like it, but you have to recognize a Pembroke can set any kind of zoning variance he wants up here, with few questions asked."

"I still can't figure out where the revenge comes in."

"Clyde is convinced the smells upset the cats."

Ron thought, My God, a pair of them. He said, "Please go on."

Flo shrugged. "There's not much more to tell. One of the scientists at the factory came up with the smoke scrubber, an improvement on anything in the line before. Pembroke Industries patented it, and were all set to go into production. We'd tried to make everything easier from the regulatory angle. Then, a month ago, Henry dug in his heels. No production, no licensing so somebody else could make it. It's his way of punishing his brother."

"What for now?"

"For making the birds go away, Ron."

"These guys are nuts."

"I won't give you an argument on that. But it is true, you know. The birds are gone. A whole section of forest—acres of trees—and not a bird around.

"I've been out there. Henry is furious, but personally I find it frightening. Not a chirp. Not a feather. Nothing."

F o u r

They were met at the door of Alpha House by a plump, smiling, middle-aged woman who introduced herself as Mrs. Everson, but whom Dickens would have called Mrs. Kumfy, or Mrs. Homebuddy, or something like that.

She went with the house. Mrs. Everson led them down the great hall, past bronze cherubs three feet tall with loudly ticking clocks in their tummies; artificial flowers made of feathers in impossible colors, kept under gleaming bell jars on top of frilly white table scarves; milk-white glass sculptures of women with serene, blank-eyed expressions on their lovely near-Greek faces no matter what unlikely posture their bodies had gotten into; and several pieces of North American and African wildlife that were being used for various decorative and utilitarian purposes (there was, for instance, an elephant's-foot umbrella stand with actual umbrellas in it. Ron could think of nothing but *The Old Curiosity Shop*. Ron and Flo Ackerman had fallen well behind the others.

"Hey, Flo," he whispered. "What the hell?"

It wasn't the most cogently asked question of Ron's detective career, but Flo understood it.

"This is a Tale from the Feud," she said. "When old Humbert, the boys' father, died, the boys divided the contents of the old house between them. Then Sophie came in and laid down the law. I got this from some women in the village who knew her when. She didn't get around, apparently, to dropping her friends until a year or so after the wedding."

Ron shrugged. "Sophie married a rich man. I assume these other women didn't. Jealousy can color memories."

"Of course it can," Flo conceded. "But the more you hear about our Sophie, the more you'll find the ring of truth in it. Anyway, she told them she told Henry, if you follow me, that she wanted *modern, ultra*-modern. A completely new house for a completely new life."

"That's a quote?"

"Secondhand, but yeah. So all the Victorian stuff had to go. Henry was all set to give it to a museum, but two things went wrong."

"I can hardly wait."

"Well, museums weren't that hot to snap this stuff up in the fifties, for one thing. There was still a lot of it around. For another, Clyde went crazy. It even got in the paper here, if you can believe that. Clyde's point was that *their mother* had bought all this . . . this . . ." Flo gestured vaguely at an exquisitely intaglioed suit of armor that Ron wouldn't have minded owning himself. Or possibly at a portrait of a child in a high-collared Sunday suit that was so awkward that Ron couldn't decide if the painter had been a major incompetent or a genius giving the world a portrait of a kid who *really hated* church.

"Their mother had bought it . . ." Ron prompted.

"Right. So, Clyde said, how dare Henry try to get rid of it? Henry's response, which also made it to the paper, was nasty. He said something to the effect that when your mother is alive and you are single, you do your best to please her. But when someone becomes a man, and marries, he must then try to please his wife. A good mother would understand, according to Henry. Of course, Henry never met my mother."

Ron grinned. "Mine either."

"The upshot of the whole thing," Flo went on, "was that Clyde took over all the tchotchkes, enough to fill a house twice this size, big as this one is, and crowded them in here."

"And Mrs. Everson and her predecessors have been dusting them ever since."

"Exactly. Henry's left them to the state of Pennsylvania in his will."

"I'm sure they'll be bowled over."

They caught up with Mrs. Everson and the Professor at the door of the study, a room paneled in oak so dark and gleaming it reminded Ron of an inside-out coffin. It was filled with deep leather furniture. There was an array of bottles on a mahogany bar in the corner.

"Please be seated," the housekeeper said. Her smile was a veritable beacon. Benedetti must have been working his Old World charm on her again. He was incorrigible in his pursuit of what he called "true Beauty—*mature* Beauty," and male chauvinist pig though the old man might be, none of the beauties in question had ever complained.

Ron was about to sink into one of the leather chairs, when a bellow came from not far away. "Mrs. Everson!" the voice said. "Bring them here! Now!"

They were led through more Victorian splendor to a room on the ground floor. Clyde Pembroke sat in front of wooden-shuttered windows at a desk whose black top was as large and smooth as a skating rink. The room was littered with trophies, the walls hung with pictures of cats overlapping complicated genetic charts.

Clyde was on the phone as the housekeeper showed them in. He looked up at them, wrinkling the purple mark on his forehead. Then he ignored them.

"Listen, Miller," he barked, "you sent me the wrong goddamn cat. No, he's beautiful. I'm sure he's a champion. Yeah, he's the right color. But he's a *rumpie*, you flaming idiot!"

He slapped the black desk to emphasize his point. "Yes, my queen is a rumpie, too. Do you think I want her to give birth to a bunch of deformed *freaks*? Do you think I *enjoy* killing kittens, you goddamn fool? I told you to send me your best red-*tailed* stud. *Tailed*, got me? Top show quality in every respect, but with a *tail*. Do you have one? If you don't, I'll look— You do. Good. Ship him here overnight. Have somebody drive all night, if you have to. My cat's not going to be in heat forever, you know, goddammit. And pick up the one you sent me. I won't be responsible. And, Miller," he concluded loudly, "*you're* paying the extra transportation."

He slammed down the phone and looked at his visitors. "What the hell did you come here so early for?"

Ron saw Flo Ackerman start to explode, think again, then think one more time before she answered. "You said five-thirty sharp, Mr. Pembroke."

Clyde Pembroke looked at his watch. "It's not even five-twenty-eight. 'Sharp' means not bent in either direction, Miss Ackerman, and I resent the interruption. Just be quiet for a minute."

Ron looked over at the Professor. A small smile bent the corners of the old man's mouth. Ron knew that expression as a sign of amusement that could easily turn to anger.

Clyde Pembroke picked up another phone on his desk. "Swantek!" he snapped. "I've been over the depreciation schemes on the new machines. I see nothing wrong with them. If my idiotic brother agrees, put them into effect. All right? Good."

A tiny *beepeepeepeep* split the air like a small but cheerful bird. Clyde Pembroke pinned the phone with his chin, pushed a button on his watch, and turned it off. ". . . And Swantek? Good job. Go home now. The business will still be here in the morning, and so will I, by God. Give my regards to Emily and the kids. Good night."

He put down the phone, leaned back, then took a deep breath. He smiled at his guests. "There," he said quietly. "That's better. When I relax, I like to relax in the knowledge that I haven't cheated on the day's work. Won't you join me in a sherry? Or anything you like, of course. I think we'll be most comfortable in the study. Mrs. Everson will show you back there; I'll join you in just a few minutes."

Mrs. Everson, was waiting outside the door for them; apparently, she'd been expecting this. Clyde Pembroke disappeared, and the three visitors followed the housekeeper back to the study.

Ron sank down on a chair that was comfortable enough to be a womb. His biggest problem was going to be staying awake. He decided to get a conversation started.

"What was that all about?" he asked.

"What?" Flo Ackerman wanted to know.

"That performance just now. Dr. Jekyll and Mr. Mellow. I mean, I've heard of good-cop, bad-cop acts, but I've never seen one person try to pull off both roles."

"That was no act," Flo said. "He means it. He starts at eight o'clock in the morning and works like a madman for ten and a half hours, driving everybody else crazy in the process. Then his watch beeps and it's all gone. Just wait until he gets back—"

Ron was about to say of *course* it was an act. If it hadn't been an act, there was no reason to summon them to the office at all. He didn't get the chance.

As if he'd been standing at the door listening, Clyde Pembroke walked in. Gone was the stiff pin-striped business suit. Now he wore gray flannel slacks, slippers, a smoking jacket of red silk, and (Ron almost goggled) an ascot.

His smile was bland and benign as he apologized for making them wait and asked what everyone was drinking. Everyone agreed to join him in a sherry. Clyde Pembroke said, "That makes it easy," went to his bar, grabbed a decanter, and poured.

If it weren't for the birthmark on his forehead, Ron would have doubted it was the same man.

Clyde passed drinks around and sat. "Well," he said. "I

must say it's an honor to meet you, Professor. I read one of your books in college."

"One of my early ones, I trust."

"What? Oh, of course, that was longer ago than I care to admit. Still, I was impressed, and I've followed your career closely. At least your public career. Your detective work."

Ron waited for the ritual correction, but to his surprise it didn't come. Ron sneaked a glance at Benedetti; the old man's face told him nothing.

Instead, the Professor said, "Thank you. I would like to ask you a few questions, if I may. If I duplicate anything Miss Ackerman or anyone else has already asked you, I apologize."

"I understand. You want to lay your own foundation. Sound approach." Clyde Pembroke put his fingertips together and pursed his lips. "Very sound. I've learned in business one can pass along authority but not responsibility. In a matter of this importance, you want to cover all the ground yourself. I approve."

"Thank you," Benedetti said. "Actually, the first thing I want to ask you is about the first telephone call we overheard during our premature arrival—for which I apologize." The Professor's head moved in the suggestion of a bow.

Clyde Pembroke waved it away. "Don't mention it. But what can that call possibly have to do with my brother's neurosis? Or the birds being missing, for that matter?"

Benedetti shrugged. "*Chi sa?* I make it a practice to satisfy my curiosity whenever possible. Knowledge is never wasted. What I learn from you may serve a need a day or a week or a year from now. Or never. At least, my curiosity will be satisfied."

"What would you like to know? Fellow just sent me the wrong cat, that's all."

"Yes. A . . . 'rumpie,' if I recall. And you requested a cat with a tail. I was under the impression the distinguishing genetic mark of the Manx cat was to have no tail."

Clyde Pembroke nodded. "Among other things," he agreed. "But the tail business can be misleading. The Manx cat, as it's known today, is probably the result of a mutation that took place on the Isle of Man, you know, off the coast of England—"

"I have been there," Benedetti said.

"Really? I'd like to visit the place myself. Maybe I will, once all this nonsense is squared away. Swantek can run the plant, and I've got good assistants at the cattery. You'll have to come see the cattery. They've got a special one on the Isle of Man, you know, royally chartered and funded, just to maintain the breed. You didn't happen to visit that while you were there, did you?"

"No. Sorry to say, my curiosity over the creatures had not yet been aroused."

"Watch it," Pembroke said, with a smile of genuine enthusiasm. "The Manx is an amazing creature, charming and strong and smart and loyal—and friendly. It even gets along with dogs. I met my first one at a friend's house about ten years ago, and I was hooked. I have one of the best operations in the East now.

"But to get back to your question. The mutation was a change in a dominant gene, but it's the kind that can be modified by the recessive gene. Forgetting colors—and Manx cats come in any color a cat can come in—you've got four kinds." He ticked them off on his fingers. "Rumpies have absolutely no tail at all, a dimple where the tail ought to be. Risers have a flap of skin there, or even a piece of cartilage or a tail vertebra or two. Only rumpies and risers are eligible to be judged as Manx in shows, you see.

"Then you've got stumpies, who have short little tails, and the tailed Manx, who have all the other Manx characteristics—and there are a lot of them—but with tails. You can't show these, but you keep the fine ones around for breeding."

"Why? Aren't you just introducing tails back into the gene pool?"

"You sure are," Pembroke said heartily. "You have to. Because if you breed two rumpies, the dominant genes reinforce each other, and you get kittens who not only have no tail, but who have deformed hind legs and can't walk, or with spina bifida, or with absolutely no control of their bowels. You have to kill them. 'Euthanize' is what the old-line breeders say, but it's heartbreaking, no matter what you call it."

"So you breed cats who lack the dominant gene into the strain," Ron said.

"Exactly. A usual litter is three to five kittens. Out of five, you might get a rumpie, a stumpie, two risers, and a tailed cat, or any other combination you can think of. But your chances are much better of having five viable kittens. You can't show them all, but you can sell them or give them away for pets.

"Actually, you *can* show your stumpies and tailed cats, but not in the Manx variety. They have to go in the AOV section, and there's no prestige in that."

"AOV?" Ron asked.

"All other varieties."

"Where is your . . . cattery, I believe you said?"

"It's on the grounds. About a quarter of a mile from here. Indoor-outdoor setup, heated and air-conditioned inside. You ought to come by, you know. One of my queens had a litter five weeks ago, and they're just about weaned. You've never seen anything cuter in your life. A rumpie, a stumpie, two risers, and a tailed cat. Simply charming."

Ron asked what he did with the cats he couldn't show.

"Well," Pembroke replied, "the really fine ones I keep for breeding, tails or no tails. Usually to cats from other catteries—too much inbreeding is a mess with the Manx. The ones who don't meet standards, I give away for pets. To kids of my employees, you know. Or just anybody responsible in town who wants a cat at the right time. You know."

"I bet the pet stores in this town just love you to pieces."

Clyde Pembroke smiled at Ron. "I don't know. They do sell a lot of cat food and cat toys because of me."

Benedetti said, "Why is the cattery so far from the house?"

"Couple of reasons. One is me. I like the little things so much, I might spend too much time with them and not enough working. The second is the cats. Tomcats like to mark their territory, especially when they can smell other toms, and things can get pretty bad out there in terms of smell. I've a good staff, and they change all the litter boxes twice a day, but it's easier to keep household staff if the cattery isn't too close to the kitchen, say."

"Do you think," Benedetti mused, "that the birds can be smelling the cats and staying away out of fear?"

Pembroke's face reddened. He looked a little more like the high-powered businessman they'd observed using the phone.

"Professor Benedetti, have you *ever* heard of a thing like that? Have you ever been to the zoo? Don't you see sparrows hopping around inside the goddam *tiger* cage, for God's sake? Besides, the area where the cattery is is *teeming* with birds. We have to be especially careful they don't get inside the cages where our cats *can* eat them. My cats get a scientifically balanced diet, and wild birds, with their bugs and parasites, are definitely *not* on it."

Benedetti gave a big grin, happy to have gotten where he was going no matter how much he provoked Pembroke. "I think that answers my question, sir, thank you. I should indeed like to visit your cattery if the chance presents itself."

"At your convenience, Professor." Pembroke was winding down, but he wasn't done yet.

"Look," he said. "No matter what my crazy brother says, I

didn't do anything to the birds. My cats didn't do anything to the birds. I *like* birds. I mean, not the way Henry does, with the binoculars and the life list and the rest, but I can tell a cardinal from an oriole, you know, and I like having them around."

I can tell the difference, too, Ron thought. Cardinals play in the National League, Orioles in the American.

"I haven't spoken to your brother," the Professor told him. "I intend to later this evening, if I can. But from what I have been told, it seems he believes the disappearance of the birds is some kind of escalation of an old feud between you."

Clyde Pembroke sipped his sherry, which reminded Ron to take another nip, too. It was nutty and smooth—good stuff.

Pembroke shook his head sadly. "The feud is—I mean, there really isn't—the feud is, if you'll pardon the expression, Miss Ackerman, a load of bullshit."

Miss Ackerman, who undoubtedly heard lots worse things every day in D.C., assured him he was forgiven.

"It's supposed to be about Sophie, right? I dated her, then he took her away and whisked her off and married her."

"That's the way the story goes," Ron acknowledged.

"It's ridiculous. Totally ridiculous. I won't deny I was mad, and that I said some harsh words. It was the first time either one of us had ever deceived the other, you see." He rubbed his forehead. "No, unless you're an identical twin yourself, you can't see. But it was that more than Sophie. So I got mad, and I stayed mad for a couple of weeks. I got over it. I was best man at the wedding. I'm godfather to Chip. It just doesn't bother me.

"But that wasn't good enough for Henry. He's always so goddam *melodramatic*. This has to be some goddam gothic novel or something, with me standing on the roof here shouting for revenge into a thunderstorm or some such ridiculous thing."

"No hard feelings at all, then?" Ron asked.

"None. Sometimes I even thought he was coming to believe that, but this bird business has wiped out any progress we've ever made. I mean, I've never actually been crass enough to *say* this to him, but he did me a favor."

Benedetti raised a brow. "A favor?"

"Well, yes. Sophie was a beautiful girl, and fun to be with, but she turned out to be lousy wife-and-mother material."

Benedetti was silent. It was a technique Ron still had trouble mastering. People have a tendency to want to fill a silence. The idea is to suppress your own urge to do it so that the subject will indulge his.

It worked again. "Sophie grew up poor. Well, not *poor*. Her father worked in the mill, and we pay damned good wages there. Never had a strike, you know. But she wasn't from the circle of girls our father encouraged us to meet. Anyway, Sophie herself was working in the steno pool in the shop when she caught my eye, and we had some fun.

"But after she married Henry, it was as if she was born Lady Sophia of Budapest or something. Twenty-seven interior decorators retired to Florida on the money she spent redecorating the inside of Omega House. I can barely stand to walk into the place now. If my father's will hadn't specified that the outside of the buildings remain as originally designed, I'm sure Henry would have had it painted pink, or something, to please her.

"But it wasn't only that. She foisted the kid off on nannies, and had no time for him while he was growing up—I swear, Chip spent almost as much time here with me and Mrs. Everson as he did with his parents. And with Jackson, of course. Jackson is the manager of the whole estate, but he lives at Omega House.

"Chip spent so little time with his parents because Sophie was always hauling Henry off to New York to watch some ballet company she'd donated his money to. Got him in the habit—he still goes off to New York at the drop of a hat, or he did until recently. Now he thinks I'll be out there shooting his birds or something if he goes away."

Clyde Pembroke shook his head grimly, lips together. He set down his sherry glass and said, "It was more than that, though. She cheated on him."

"Indeed," Benedetti said. "Did he know?"

"Probably not. Or he willed himself not to know. He was probably the only one who didn't. I certainly didn't tell him, though she even made a pass at me one time. Henry was out bird-watching or something. 'For old times' sake,' she said."

Pembroke looked up, expecting a question. He didn't get it, but he answered it anyway. "And for the record, no, I did not. I'm no monk, but I'm proud to say I've never dallied with a married woman. And how the hell any of this is going to get the smoke scrubbers built is beyond me. What are you, Professor, a hypnotist?"

"You have been most helpful, Mr. Pembroke." Benedetti rose and extended a hand. Their host rose too, and shook it.

"Anything I can do to help," Pembroke said.

"*Va bene,*" Benedetti said. "There is something."

"Name it."

"The request is simple. Just allow me and Mr. Gentry— and his wife, when she joins us—to stay here at Alpha House while we look into the matter."

"You want to stay *here*?"

"If at all possible," the Professor said, as if asking to use the bathroom. Then he *did* ask to use the bathroom. Two of them. He wanted rooms with private baths.

"We will take our meals with you or separately, as you prefer, Mr. Pembroke. The expenses of our stay will be reimbursed by the Environmental Protection Agency, won't they, Miss Ackerman?"

Ron suppressed a smile as he looked at Flo. A woman who

dealt habitually with congressmen must have seen her share of chutzpah, but this was something new. She stared at the Professor for a moment, then closed her mouth, swallowed, and said, "Of course."

"Well, if it will help get this business squared away . . ." Pembroke was having a hard time mustering enthusiasm.

"It will, I assure you. Of course, if you find it a hardship, we can see if your brother can accommodate us."

Ron could almost see the wheels turning in Clyde Pembroke's head. If they wind up at Henry's house, Henry will be propagandizing against me day and night, and who needs that, how much bother can they be . . . ?

"No, no inconvenience at all," Pembroke said. "When would you like to move in?" Pembroke decided he didn't like the sound of "move in." He tried again. "When would you like to come over?"

"Tomorrow afternoon will be fine," the Professor assured him.

"I may not be here. I like to go to the factory a couple of times each week. I don't think Henry's been there five times since he got married." He sighed. Ron pegged him as a man who liked to think he bore his crosses patiently—outside of working hours, at least.

"Thank you again, Mr. Pembroke. We will go see your brother now."

"Just follow the gravel road to the left. When you come to the fork in the road, go right. That'll bring you right up to the front of Omega House."

"Actually, I mean for us to walk. I wish to see the area from which the birds have vanished."

• • •

There was a well-marked path through the woods toward the other house. In some places, it was even covered with white gravel, but mostly it was mud. The sky was overcast, and the sun was going down. It wasn't raining, but there was enough mist in the air to turn the trees a dripping leathery black in the fading light.

"If I'd known we were going to do this tonight, *Maestro*," Ron said, "I would have worn tougher shoes."

"Have I not managed to teach you that investigation is an often disagreeable chore, my friend? You will note Miss Ackerman is not complaining."

"Miss Ackerman is being polite," Ron suggested.

"Miss Ackerman," retorted Miss Ackerman, "is used to walking around toxic waste dumps on short notice. This is almost a pleasure."

But Ron was tired, hungry, and in a teasing mood. "Nero Wolfe would never start tramping through the woods in twilight."

"No," Benedetti conceded. "He would remain home in comfort reading a book while his assistant went tramping through the woods at twilight. At least you have me here to complain to. Besides, Nero Wolfe is a character in a book. Now *sta' zitto*, I am trying to think."

Ron kept quiet. He wanted to think, too. This was not the kind of case the Professor usually interested himself in. Usually, there were some atrocious murders, and all Benedetti had to do was catch the killer. This was different. There were no deaths; nobody had even been hurt. The question here was what the hell was it exactly that *was* going on?—and it was mildly unnerving.

Ron decided he was in no shape to worry about anything now. In addition to fatigue and hunger (and he'd have to make a point about dinner to Benedetti very soon now—the Professor, it seemed, could live off the vibrations of his own genius when he felt like it), Ron felt a very real resentment at not having been able to take a day or two off before plunging into this thing. About not having had a chance to see Janet.

They slogged along in silence. The only sounds were the crunch of shoes on gravel, the squish of shoes on mud, and the occasional cry of a bird.

Then there were no cries of birds.

"We are here," Benedetti said. "Listen."

Ron listened. He listened until he could hear himself breathing. He could hear Benedetti and Flo breathing. There was the occasional drip of water from a wet bough.

Ron smelled something. "My God," he whispered. "I *am* going nuts."

"What is it, *amico*?" Benedetti demanded.

"Grape," Ron said. "I smell grape again."

F i v e

Benedetti frowned at him. "Are you all right, *amico*?"

"I don't know. Don't you smell it?"

"Yes, I smell it."

"Really?"

"Ronald, I do not humor people, as you should well know."

"If it's any consolation," Flo Ackerman said, "I smell it, too."

"Good."

"But why are you so upset, *amico*? Surely one might expect to smell a sweet flavoring in the near vicinity of an ice-cream factory, no?"

"Ice-cream factory," Ron muttered. "Of course. Well, I certainly feel like an idiot. Sorry, Flo. Sorry, Professor. I guess I'm just out of it today."

"We will soon be done for the day," the Professor said.

"Your mouth to God's ears," Ron said.

Flo Ackerman laughed. "My mother says that all the time. Are you Jewish, by any chance?"

"No such luck," he said.

The Professor was back concentrating on the matter at hand. "It is no exaggeration. The birds are gone, from this area at least."

"They've just moved," Ron said. "That's probably why there are so many around the cattery now, according to Clyde Pembroke, at least."

"Obviously. The question is why did they go, eh?"

"I can't answer that one, *Maestro*."

"Neither can I. Yet. Let us press on."

A couple of hundred feet down the trail, Flo Ackerman gave a little scream and fell down.

Ron ran to help her. "Are you all right?" he asked.

"I don't know," Flo said. "I twisted my ankle."

"Perhaps, *amico*, I should stay with Miss Ackerman while you get help," Benedetti suggested.

"Oh, no, Professor," Flo protested.

Ron peered closely at the ankle. "It doesn't look too bad. Want to try it?"

"Sure," she said. She held out her hand and Ron helped her to her feet. She tried to walk, wobbled a little, gave them a brave smile. "I can make it, if we don't go too fast. And if you give me a hand." She took Ron's arm, and they marched on.

It was only minutes later that the forest parted in front of them, and they were walking toward the front door of Omega House. When they were about twenty feet along the flagstone walk that led to the door, a figure loomed up out of the shrubbery to their left. It was tall and lean, and hard to make out in the last of the dusk. In its right hand, it held a small sickle that gleamed even in the gathering darkness.

Flo screamed, jumped back into Ron, and held on. Ron was trying to shed her, to have his arms free to deal with the apparition. He was about to throw her to the ground, not gently, when he heard Benedetti bark, "*Amico*, no!"

The noise seemed to quiet Flo down. She let go of Ron and peered.

"Mr. Jackson," she said. "You startled me. Especially with that thing in your hand."

Jackson's voice was soft and rich. "Sorry," he said. He put the tool behind his back, as if somehow ashamed of it, then walked forward.

As he came closer, Ron could see that Jackson was about the same age as the Professor. His brown face was heavily lined, and the lines emphasized whatever emotion his face was expressing at the moment. Right now, they were expressing cautious amusement. Despite his age, the wedge of hair that stood up from his head was a shiny black.

The Professor stepped forward, hand extended. "Good evening. I am Niccolo Benedetti. This is my associate, Ronald Gentry, and I believe you know Miss Ackerman."

"Yes, I do." Jackson spoke to her. "I'm Jackson, estate manager here. The gardeners always seem to be slovenly with the grass between the flagstones. The only way to do it is to get down there with a sickle, you know. So I was bringing the work up to par." Now he spoke to all of them. "I'm sorry if I startled you. We're all mighty glad you're here. The atmosphere is going to be a whole lot better if you can figure out how to get the birds back."

"We shall do our best, Mr. Jackson," the Professor reassured him.

Just then, the light came on over the front door. The door itself opened a second later, and a young, pleasant-faced man popped his balding head out and said, "I thought I heard something out here. Everything all right, Mr. Jackson?"

"Just fine," Jackson said. "Our visitors are here. If you don't mind showing them in, I'll go clean things up in the shed."

The young man, who had to be Chip Pembroke, told him sure, and emerged to usher his visitors to the door.

Once inside, he took jackets (the servant-master relationships in these parts were very informal, Ron reflected) and hung them up on a device that looked like an octopus making love to a Russian samovar.

"Hi, Flo," Chip said. "Uncle Clyde said you'd be around. You must be Professor Benedetti and Gentry."

Ron admitted it.

"Well, I'm awfully glad you're here. I'm Chip," he said, offering handshakes. He looked like his Uncle Clyde (and therefore, presumably, his father) only from the cheekbones up. His eyes had Clyde's shrewd look to them, and the strange greenish glint behind the brown. From there down, he was someone else entirely, undoubtedly Sophie. He had the kind of looks that can be perky and pretty on a woman but tend to look unfinished and callow in a man. His handshake was firm and dry, though, and there was a quiet confidence in his voice.

"Actually," he went on, "Humbert Pembroke the second, if you can stand it. The best thing my mother ever did for me was to call me 'Chip.'"

"Nice to meet you," Ron said. "Listen, Flo twisted her ankle out in the woods—"

"You came through the *woods*? In the dark?"

"It wasn't dark when we started. We wanted to check if this bird business was real."

Chip offered a strained smile. "And you found out, didn't you? Spooky, no?"

"Very."

Chip Pembroke took Flo's arm from Ron and led her to an orange leather divan. At least Ron thought it was a divan. Nothing in this room was exactly the shape or exactly the color you'd feel comfortable with. Right in front of the divan, for instance, was what Ron supposed was a coffee table consisting of three cones of chromium holding up a liver-colored plastic tabletop in the shape of an artist's palette, complete with thumbhole. Ron guessed it was a sobriety test. When you put your drink down on the hole, it was time to stop for the night.

The whole thing was very fifties. Not like anything anybody actually had in their *homes* in the fifties; the kind of stuff you found in style magazines, where some designer had to carry things to their extremes. The whole place was filled with chrome and leather and plastic, pastels and Day-Glo colors, shiny surfaces and geometric textures.

Ron suspected that Sophie had done to the entire house what some women did with their clothes and hair and makeup. Lucille Ball became well known in the 1940s, and her appearance was stuck in the forties for the rest of her life. Ron's mother came of age in the early sixties, and she wore long, straight hair to this very day. To the late Sophie Havelka, from the wrong side of the tracks, this house had been the height of style during the period of her greatest triumph, and she froze it in time.

It was, Ron thought, more alien and uncomfortable than the jumble of Victorian monstrosities in Alpha House could ever be.

The room they were in was a huge space. Obviously, one or more of Sophie's decorators had earned a piece of his retirement money by knocking out a few of the walls. Now, you could shoot a 1950s science fiction movie in the place.

• • •

As she lay on the divan, Flo wondered what the hell she thought she was doing. She'd twisted her ankle, all right, but it was nothing, the pain over in a minute. Why was she acting like an invalid, for God's sake? she asked herself. But she knew why. She was doing it, or at least had done it, because she wanted to get hold of Ron Gentry's body. She'd settled for his arm. Even through her jacket and his, he'd radiated a warm sensation.

She told herself she was being a fool; the man had shown no interest in her at all past a friendly concern, and he was *married* to one of the best friends she'd ever had. She'd just have to stop this foolishness right now.

But as she sat up and wiggled out of her jacket, she wondered if Ron Gentry was watching.

• • •

Chip Pembroke looked to Ron to be about eighteen years old, marked up from sixteen only because of the thinning brown hair he wore slicked over a growing bald spot. Chip wasn't fat exactly, but seemed as if he were headed in that direction. He had an incipient double chin and looked soft to the touch. Ron supposed that was tolerable in an ice cream magnate.

His clothes—button-down shirt with a tiny red check, white chinos, gray wool socks, and penny loafers (no pennies)—and his gee-whiz attitude toward the Professor and Ron himself added to the illusion of youth. In fact, Chip was past forty, some years older than Ron himself.

After getting repeated assurances that Flo was fine, didn't need a doctor, didn't want an aspirin, was, in fact, about to get up off the divan and tap-dance, Chip turned to his other guests.

"Greetings! Welcome to Omega House. Sounds like a fraternity, doesn't it? I suppose you want to see Dad. I'll go get him in a second. Please, sit down. Want anything to drink?"

The Professor and Flo declined with thanks. Ron said, "You wouldn't happen to have a grape soda, would you?"

Chip looked at him with something close to horror.

Ron grinned in spite of himself. "Just trying a long shot. I've had the urge all day."

"No, I . . . I'm afraid we don't. We've got Coke, and Seven-Up, and tonic and seltzer. And liquor, of course."

"Seven-Up will be fine."

"Okay, just a sec." A few moments later, Chip returned with a glass. "Actually, it's Sprite."

"That's fine," Ron said. "Thanks."

"I'll go get Dad. Take good care of Flo. She and I have been trying to bring those two old coots together, and I'm glad to see reinforcements."

"We will do what we can," the Professor said.

"Not that I want you to be too hard on my father, either."

The Professor repeated, "We will do what we can," this time with a gentle smile.

So much, Ron thought, for not humoring anybody.

Henry Pembroke returned without his son. Clyde's twin brother walked down the main stairs. They were in the same place here as they were in Alpha House, but the magnificent marble had been replaced by a construction of steel struts and white wood. It didn't look strong enough to hold a Slinky, let alone a man, but Chip had ascended, and Henry came down, without so much as a wobble.

Henry Pembroke wore royal-blue sweatpants and sweat-shirt, and had a fluffy white towel wrapped around his neck. He was sweating profusely, and he wiped his face from time to time. He was considerably thinner than his twin, and that made him seem a little taller, but he probably wasn't. Still, they were enough alike that if it weren't for the forceps mark on Clyde's forehead, it would be impossible to tell them apart if you didn't have them side by side.

Henry's purple mark was on his left forearm, above the wrist. Ron noticed it when Henry raised the towel to wipe his face. Not too useful as identification. It would be easy to keep that covered up.

Pembroke smiled and gave a slight nod of his head. "Miss Ackerman. Professor Benedetti. Mr. Gentry." His voice was softer than his brother's, with a slight rasp to it. "Please for-give me for the way I look; I was working out. I didn't know when you'd be here."

"It's quite all right, Mr. Pembroke," the Professor told him. "Neither did we. But I did want to get to you today, if only to reassure you of my commitment to the case."

Henry pulled a metal-and-plastic chair around and sat on it. "I understand it was the birds that made you decide to help here. Wait till you see."

"I have seen. We came here from Alpha House through the woods."

"Unnerving, isn't it? Worse than unnerving. People forget how important nature is, even in the background of our lives. To stand in that part of the woods is . . . bizarre." He wiped himself with the towel again and shook his head in a quick shivering motion. "It's almost supernatural, as if there's been a curse put on the place."

"Do you believe that to be the case?"

Benedetti's voice was soft as he asked the question. Ron knew the Professor loved it when people started ascribing the phenomena he looked into to supernatural causes.

There'd be no joy on that score this time, though.

"Oh, of course not," Henry Pembroke said firmly. "Guess where my broker is now?"

The Professor was unfazed by the seeming non sequitur. "I couldn't begin to."

"He's in France. Mont St.-Denis. He likes to beat the rush for skiing, you know. He wrote to me last week, when I mentioned we'd asked you to come here, that the place is still buzzing about how you unmasked the 'werewolf.'"

Henry Pembroke sat back in the chair. "No, I don't really think anything supernatural is going on. Still," he murmured, "it would be nice to know how he's doing it."

"By 'he' you mean your brother, I suppose."

"Who else? That's why I'm so glad you're here, Professor. It will take a genius to trap him. We're supposed to be identical twins, but there is a major difference. *Two* major differences.

"The first one is that Clyde is brilliant. Absolutely brilliant. There is a strain of high intelligence in our family. Our father had it; Clyde has it. People laugh at me when I say this, but my son Chip has it—it's just hidden under his inherent good nature. But, somehow, I don't have it.

"But in Clyde, the intelligence goes along with a fierce competitiveness. I won something he wanted only once, and he has hated me ever since."

Ron was sure they were going to get the Sophie story again, this time from the other side, but the Professor double-crossed him.

Benedetti said, "You said there were two differences."

"Yes, I did. The other difference is this: I have a conscience; Clyde has none, none at all."

There was a sudden pounding on the great front door, someone literally smashing something against the oak. They could make out a man's voice, screaming, on the verge of hysteria.

"Let me in, or, by God, Henry, I'll *burn* this place down with you in it! You goddam evil bastard! Open this goddam door!"

Chip came running down the stairs. He looked a question at his father, who sighed. Chip ran on and opened the front door. He said, "Uncle Clyde—," then got steamrollered out of the way.

Clyde Pembroke came stomping into the room, ignoring all the clashing colors and rampant modernity. He was carrying a cardboard box. He thumped it down on a table, then, shaking with rage, he walked over to Henry, shaking a fist in his face and bellowing, "I've put up with a lot of shit from you because of who you are, but this time you've gone too far. If anything like this ever happens again, little brother, I'll kill you. Do you hear me? *I'll kill you!*"

He spun on his heel and stormed out.

It was only after the door had slammed behind him that it occurred to Ron to move. He walked to the box and lifted a flap. "Oh, Jesus," he said, and closed it again.

"What is inside?" Benedetti demanded.

"A cat," Ron said. "A kitten, actually."

"Dead?"

"Oh, yeah. Very. Somebody crushed its skull."

Ron could feel their breath on him as the others crowded around the box. Flo Ackerman made a surprisingly feline whimper of her own, then turned away abruptly. Chip, his eyes wide, kept breathing, "Oh, geez, what a thing," to the universe at large.

Henry was silent. He stared into the box. He showed no expression, but every three seconds or so, a dark little tongue tip darted out and moistened his thin lips. He might have been doing anything from suppressing tears to gloating at the death of a potential bird killer.

Benedetti, as usual, remained unflappable. "I think," he said, "I'd like to have a few more words with Mr. Clyde Pembroke. Fetch him back, Ronald, if you would."

Ron was already moving by the time the Professor finished talking. He knew he'd have to move fast to catch the cat fancier, and he was glad of a chance to burn off some adrenaline.

Ron Gentry did not consider himself a cat lover. As a matter of fact, his experience with felines had led him to consider them royal pains in the ass. He'd had a girlfriend (before he met Janet) who'd watch her cat torture a mouse to death and eat it, polish off a can of gourmet cat food, then knock over a garbage can to get some old chicken skin before she scooped him up and kissed him on the top of the head and called him poopsie-woopsie. The relationship hadn't lasted too long.

He knew that the cat was doing what came naturally, but that didn't mean he had to like it. Or to put up with calling the author of such behavior poopsie-woopsie, either.

But there was nothing natural about what had been done to the animal in the box. It was a deliberate act of cruelty committed by a creature (i.e., a human—no other animals crushed skulls and left whole bodies around) who was supposed to know better. It made Ron angry.

He caught Clyde Pembroke just about to get into his black Lincoln Town Car.

"Mr. Pembroke! Wait!"

Pembroke slammed the car door without getting in and leaned against the Lincoln with his arms folded, tapping a foot in impatience. His eyes were narrow, and his lips were tight.

"What is it, Gentry?" he demanded.

"The Professor would like you to step back inside, please."

"I am never going back inside that house again. I made that promise before, and it took something like this to make me break it. If I go in there again, I won't be responsible for what I do. I swear, I want to kill him!"

"Don't you want to help the Professor find out who did this?"

"I know who did it!"

"Right. Just like your brother knows who chased the birds away."

"That's entirely different."

"Why? He blames you for something, says you did it out of perversity and peeve. Now you're blaming him for something, and saying he did it for the same reasons.

"Let me tell you something," Ron continued bluntly. "The security on this estate stinks. I could bring a marching band through here at regular intervals, and neither you nor your brother would know a damned thing about it. Anybody in the world could be scaring birds and bashing cats, but you two would rather take it out on each other."

Ron leaned so close to Pembroke that the man's breath fogged his glasses. "And as long as I'm at it, let me tell you something else. If you two crybabies weren't standing between the rest of your fellow citizens and cleaner air, you could feud to your heart's content."

Pembroke stared into Ron's eyes for a tense moment. At last he demanded, "Are you done?"

"For now. Coming inside?"

"Well, hell, I'd better, hadn't I?" Clyde started walking for the door. "I hope you find an opportunity to tell my brother off like that at some point. He's not used to it, either."

Ron grinned. "I'll make it a point. And don't worry about not being responsible. If you start to get out of control, I'll sit on your head."

"You wouldn't have said that when I was your age."

"Probably not," Ron said.

"I don't like people who abuse animals, Gentry. I just don't."

He's probably against man-eating sharks and the bombing of orphanages, too, Ron thought. Still, Clyde was getting his temper back, and he was under control, if not calm, when they went back inside.

By now, the box was closed again. It had been placed on some open sheets of newspaper on a pale-green kidney-shaped table. Benedetti stood by the box. The green tinge on all the other faces matched the table.

"Thank you for returning, Mr. Pembroke. I have persuaded your brother to agree to a truce if you will do the same," the Professor said.

"I do. I think I already have. Mr. Gentry can be very, ah, persuasive himself. I just want to say that if *I* have unjustly accused anybody, *I* apologize. If."

"Noted," Benedetti said dryly. "Now, sir, we need to avail ourselves of your expertise in the matter of cats, and to ask you some general questions."

Clyde Pembroke nodded wearily. "May I sit?"

Benedetti looked at Henry Pembroke, who nodded to Chip, who said, "Sure, Uncle Clyde."

"Now," the Professor said, "where and when did you find this animal?"

"Near the path, not far from the cattery. I decided to go out there a little while after you left, to see if everything was all right. And maybe just to visit the cats, you know. Then I saw . . . this . . . lying by the edge of the pathway. I saw it lying there, in the half-light. I went to it to see if I could do it any good. I took out my pocket flashlight and saw . . . what's in the box now."

"Is it one of your cats?" the Professor asked.

"What? One of *mine*?"

"Your cattery is the most abundant immediate source of cats, *non è vero*? It seems a natural question."

"No, no. It's not one of mine. Look at it, it's not even a Manx."

"Forgive me. I see it has a tail, but I have learned only today that that does not disqualify it as a member of the breed."

Clyde Pembroke popped up from his chair. "Here," he said, "let me show you."

He walked over to the box and opened it. After a look inside, he turned to the Professor and said, "Goddamn whoever did this. I admit I was hasty." He said it a little louder. "I admit I was hasty, but I just saw red. Thank the Lord this wasn't one of my cats; I might have come over here with a gun."

Ron watched Henry while Clyde spoke. The bird-watcher took it deadpan, eyes a little narrowed, head tilted to one side.

"You can see," Clyde told Benedetti, "that the body from end to end makes a longer rectangle than a Manx does. Manx cats are very boxy. Also, a Manx's hind legs are considerably longer than its forelegs. This cat's are more or less the same."

Clyde let out a deep breath and closed the box. "Even if this had been a Manx, it almost certainly wouldn't have been one of mine. I specialize in dark-orange cats, what we call red ones. This poor thing is a gray tabby. Color in any cat never breeds one hundred percent true, but a gray tabby Manx is very unlikely. Besides, I would have known about it."

"Where would you guess this cat has come from?"

"Anywhere. Probably a stray. They wander into woods; always have. There was one Henry and I used to play with when we were boys."

Again, Ron looked at the brother. Henry didn't appear overwhelmed with nostalgia.

"Our father didn't let us have any pets; we fed a stray cat that wandered onto the grounds. This was when we lived in the old house way on the other side of the estate. Burned down in 1973. Nothing left there but a few outbuildings. As Gentry pointed out, our security here—we've never really felt the need for it, to tell you the truth—wouldn't keep a marching band out, let alone a kitten."

"Yeah," Ron said. "I suggest we do something about that."

"What do you mean?" It was the first time Henry Pembroke had said a word since Ron had come back inside.

"Assuming, for the sake of argument, that neither of you two gentlemen is tormenting the other, somebody is tormenting you both. Getting rid of the birds, however it was done, could be a nasty prank; smashing that cat's head is the work of a psycho. I suggest that tomorrow we get somebody from the police department up here and *all of us*, meaning the police officer, me, and both of you, sit down and work something out."

The twins worked their jaws and made faces as if they were chewing soap. Chip looked surprised, skeptical, and hopeful, all at once. Flo was so thrilled, she did everything short of clasping her hands in front of her bosom and squealing.

Finally, Clyde got it swallowed and spoke up. "I guess I got the craziest. Tonight, that is. So I'll say it first. I'll go along, if you really think it's necessary."

Ron turned to Henry. "How about you?"

Henry worked on it a long time. Seemed like hours; it was probably forty-five seconds. However long it took, it was almost long enough for Clyde to lose his temper again. His face was getting dangerously pink.

Finally, Henry said, "All right."

"Fine," Ron said. "Find out when it's convenient for the cop." That eliminated one thing they might decide to fight about. Now there was just one left. Where were they going to do this? Ron figured the representative of the law would look askance at meeting in the middle of the lawn somewhere, and to suggest either of their houses was to invite trouble.

Chip came to the rescue. "You can meet in my factory," he said. "When I had the thing built, I put in a small conference room that's never been used. I've got a slide projector in there and everything."

"Great," Ron said heartily. "That's settled. Miss Ackerman will know how to reach us."

"But—," Clyde Pembroke began.

The Professor cut him off. No sense Henry knowing before the meeting that he and Ron were moving in with Clyde. "That, I think, will be all for the night. Perhaps, Mr. Pembroke, you will oblige us with a lift back to Alpha House. Miss Ackerman's car is there."

S e v e n

"Sorry," Flo Ackerman said as Ron's head bounced off the ceiling. "That was a bad one."

"I don't think they have any good ones." Ron sounded about the same way he would if he were being mixed up in a cement truck. "Did you ever notice," he said, complete with quaverings in his voice as they went over bumps and through potholes, "that the richer somebody is, the worse their driveway? Remember Benac's château in France, Professor? You had to have an army tank to get in there."

"That, my friend," the Professor said from the back seat, "is because the rich need not make it easy for people to come to them. Money has a magnetic power all its own."

"I just feel sorry for the people who work in Clyde's cattery. Or in Chip's ice-cream factory, for that matter."

Benedetti grunted. "It might be more appropriate for you to feel sorry for the American taxpayers who will have to replace this car."

"This is my own car," Flo Ackerman said grimly.

In the rearview mirror, Ron caught the hint of a grin on Benedetti's face.

"My apologies," the old man said.

"It's all right. We're almost at the paved road."

"Good," Ron said. It came out "Goo-oo-ood," as the car hit two deep potholes close together.

They passed the vine-covered columns that marked the entrance to the Pembroke compound, and emerged onto the (relatively) smooth county road.

"That's better," Flo Ackerman said. "Thanks."

"I didn't do anything," Ron said.

"Are you kidding? You were great. That was the nicest those two have been to each other since I've heard of them. You've got them talking to each other."

"Excuse me, Miss Ackerman," the Professor said from the back seat. "They didn't talk to each other."

"No?" She thought it over. "No. I guess not. But they're more or less *promising* to. This is the best things have looked in this situation in months, and you did it all in one afternoon."

"I just pointed out a couple of obvious facts, that's all," Ron said.

"They *agreed* about something."

"Throughout history," Benedetti said, "the evocation of the common enemy has been a powerful method for unifying warring factions. Perhaps the most powerful."

Ron was exasperated. "*Maestro.* I didn't evoke anything, okay?"

"Not purposefully, perhaps, Ronald. But Miss Ackerman is right; you did get them to entertain the possibility that their enemy is someone outside the bonds of blood. That must be a welcome possibility, especially for two beings who have grown from the same egg."

"Look at it this way," Flo said. Even in the darkness, Ron could see her eyes gleam. "If Clyde and Henry can agree on a security plan, there's no reason why they can't agree to expand their factory and help the environment with the smoke scrubber. I get their signatures on a government contract, the problem is solved, and we can all go home."

Benedetti cleared his throat. "I am sorry to disappoint you, Miss Ackerman, but I was not engaged to get anyone's signature on a government contract. Achieving that may mean the end of your job, but not of mine."

"But all we need—"

"Forgive me, but I am indifferent to what you need, or to what the Environmental Protection Agency needs. I plan to fulfill my own needs."

"I . . . I don't know what you mean, Professor."

"I mean that for my self-esteem as a man, I need to do what I have said I will do. For my work as a philosopher, I need to study the evil that has been done in this place."

The Professor leaned back in his seat. "The birds are still gone, Miss Ackerman. I will not leave this town until I have learned why."

They drove on in silence.

• • •

Things were cheery again by the time they pulled up at the inn. Flo parked the car and said, "Just let me freshen up, and I insist on buying dinner. The restaurant here is pretty darned good."

"Is it open?"

"Of course it's open. It's only twenty after eight."

Ron looked at his watch. "My God, so it is. I feel as if I've been up forever."

"I am sorry, *amico*," the Professor said, "you will be awake for some time yet."

Ron groaned. The old man turned to Flo. "I am sorry, Miss Ackerman, but we must decline your kind offer. My friend and I have much work to do, and we must get started before he falls asleep on me. Perhaps another time; maybe even to-morrow. If fortune is with us, we may be celebrating the successful completion of your assignment, if not of mine. Except I insist that we must pay."

We meaning me, Ron thought. Benedetti never paid for anything.

"No, no," Flo said. "*I* insist. Think of it as a chance to get

some of your tax money back. The thanks of a grateful nation and all that."

Benedetti smiled warmly. "Well, since you put it that way,
we accept."

On the way to their room, Ron kept wondering what sort
of work they had to do. Benedetti was not a great one for sitting around discussing things. He was more likely to hide in
a room by himself and paint. As the case went on, the paint-
ings got more and more abstract. When you couldn't, at first
glance, decide what the hell they were, that meant the old
man had figured the thing out.

Flo had gotten them the best accommodations in the
place: a three-room suite, two baths, very nice. The furniture
looked like Real Furniture rather than Hotel Furniture, and
the bed looked comfortable. In fact, if he hadn't been so
hungry (he should have remembered about the candy bar
back in Maine), it would have looked too comfortable to re-
sist. As it was, Ron took off his jacket and tie and shoes,
emptied his pockets, and went to join the Professor in the
sitting room.

The old man was on the phone to room service, enumer-
ating items. As far as Ron could tell, he would have achieved
the same result in less time just by telling the person on the
other end of the phone to bring up two of everything.

Ron said as much to the old man. "Which would be fine,"
he continued, "except what are you going to eat?"

"I shall content myself with a crumb here and a crust
there, *amico.*"

"What kind of work is it we have to do?" Ron asked.

"It can wait."

"I can't. It's only starvation that's keeping me awake. I'll
probably pass out in the food. Maybe I better go take a shower while we wait."

"Call your wife first."

Ron looked at him.

"You didn't have a chance to when you first arrived, and since then, we have been busy. Janet is probably sick with worry. Use the telephone for one of its nobler purposes. Put the woman's mind at rest."

Ron couldn't argue with the logic or the sentiment, but he wished he knew where the latter had come from. Benedetti had never been what you'd call the domestically oriented type.

Ron picked up the phone, figured out what the hell he had to do to get hold of the phone company he wanted, dialed that number, dialed his home number, listened for the bong and the tape thanking him, dialed his credit card number, then waited for the ringing to start.

"Be quicker to send a letter," he muttered.

Janet picked up on the second ring. He told her why it had taken him so long to call, and she immediately forgave him. She asked him how things were going.

"Weird," he told her. "We could really use some psychological insights. When are you getting down here?"

"Tomorrow," Janet said, and the word in Ron's ears was full of joy and possibility.

"Tomorrow, that's great. I've been missing you."

Benedetti pointed to himself and reached for the phone. Ron was surprised but said, "Hold on a second. The Professor wants to talk to you."

Ron heard his wife's voice say, "The *Professor*?" as he handed over the phone.

Benedetti put the receiver to his ear. "Ah, dear Janet, it is a pleasure, as always, to hear your voice. Am I correct in my impression that you are joining us tomorrow? No, on the contrary, I believe it to be an excellent idea. Your old friend is attempting to seduce your husband, and he is too much a *gabbia testa* to notice."

E i g h t

Janet Higgins was amazed at her own peace of mind. She didn't even mind the cramped airline seat on the short hop between Sparta, New York, and Scranton, Pennsylvania. Almost as tall as her husband, she usually spent commercial flights chasing fugitive pains around her various cramped-up joints.

Of course, Janet was honest enough with herself to admit that the cramped feeling and the pains were probably by-products of her general dislike of flying. Ron was never troubled with them.

Janet was always honest with herself—at least as honest as anybody whose constant companion was that master trickster, the human subconscious, could be. She considered it her duty as a psychologist. She knew that it was impossible to insist that you yourself be neurosis-free before you tried to help someone else, but it was incumbent in a trained professional, she felt, at least to be aware of your kinks.

So she drifted into her habit of being honest with herself. Why was she so happy on this trip, even though the plane had been taking off into a cloudy sky and had a good chance of running into turbulence?

She wished she hadn't thought of the turbulence. She signaled for a flight attendant, who materialized like a genie from a lamp. "White wine, please?" A little wine always helped to calm her down.

Before the flight attendant could turn away, Janet said, "No! I mean, I changed my mind. I'm sorry. Just a club soda, if it's okay?"

The club soda was forthcoming. Janet sipped at it daintily. That was silly of me, she thought. No more wine for a while.

So forget the turbulence. Why so cheery?

Well, for one thing, she'd been looking forward to this trip since Benedetti decided to go. For another, even more than usual, she was bursting with news for Ron.

And best of all, the now-glamorous Flo Ackerman had been, according to the Professor, making passes at her husband, and he hadn't even noticed it. That was good. That was better than good. Janet had spent the early years of her marriage to Ron not exactly *not* trusting him, just having difficulty believing how a hunk like him could be contented with her. The fact that he professed to be prostrated by her beauty, and the fact that he loved the fact that "she didn't look like anybody else," were not calculated to solve the problem. A woman who has felt lonely and isolated since girlhood *wants* to look like everybody else. She *wants* to be thought conventionally pretty, even while she knows she's not.

Until, of course, she wises up. Janet wasn't sure she had, yet, not completely. She still didn't exactly understand Ron's devotion to her, but she had come to believe it. And since pleasing him made her happy, and he was manifestly pleased with her the way she was, she'd come to accept herself, flat chest, bumpy nose, mousy hair, and all.

Now she believed it even more. She was astonished to find she wasn't even very angry with Flo. She was more sorry for her.

Last night, the Professor had said, "Please, *cara amica*, do not get the wrong impression. There is no danger that Ronald will succumb to the importunings."

"None, Professor?"

"The Word of Niccolo Benedetti. That is not the problem."

In the background, she could hear Ron: "*Maestro*, what are you talking about?"

"What is the problem, Professor?" Janet asked.

"The problem is the possibility that in not noticing, Ronald will unintentionally encourage the approaches to escalate, until they cannot be cut off without damage to Miss Ackerman's self-esteem. She is an efficient worker, and not brainless. It will help our task here if she is not upset."

Even then, Janet had been more amused than anything else. Poor Flo. Of all the times to come on to Ron, she picked about the worst. And it would be the absolute worst, as soon as Janet got there.

"Don't worry, Professor. As I told Ron, I'll be there tomorrow. I'll take care of it."

"Good. I will be glad of your presence for other reasons as well. I have an intuition that the strange things are just beginning here. Now I will give you back to your husband. Travel safely."

Ron took the phone. "Janet, really. I haven't—"

"I know, dear. Don't worry about it. Even if she were, and you wanted to, I'll be there tomorrow, so she wouldn't get close to you."

"No," Ron muttered, "but I'm going to get close to you."

"Mm-hmm. And don't you forget it."

Janet was smiling when she hung up.

So, the plane was coming in for a landing at—she glanced at her watch—about two-thirty on a Saturday afternoon. Ron would have had his meeting with the brothers and the police about the security on the estate (he'd mentioned that when they were deciding what plane she'd take). He'd take her back to the hotel, she'd tell him the big news, they'd give the Professor some money and send him to the movies (actually, the Professor had a sixth sense for knowing when he wasn't needed), and she and Ron would disappear for a late matinee.

No wonder she was enjoying the plane trip.

The plane stopped. She grabbed her bag and went into the terminal.

Ron wasn't waiting at the gate. He wasn't waiting in the waiting room, either. Okay, traffic or something. Nothing to worry about.

Janet found a phone, got a coin and a phone number from her purse, and called the inn. Neither Mr. Gentry nor Professor Benedetti was in. Did she care to leave a message?

"If they check in, just tell them I've arrived, and I'm at the airport. They're probably on their way already."

Well, she reflected as she hung up, Ron probably was. The Professor wasn't a big one for meeting people at airports.

The place here wasn't so big that Ron could be wandering around, missing her. The thing to do was to take a seat and wait by her gate until Ron showed up. He'd probably be there any minute.

She found a bench nearby, sat down, pulled out the new James Herriot, and was swept off to postwar Yorkshire while she waited patiently.

After a half hour, she was waiting less patiently.

After an hour, she waited much less patiently.

After an hour and fifteen minutes, she was torn by mixed feelings. Half the time, she felt she'd been forgotten and was furious, and half the time, she was convinced that Ron's battered body was lying under a car wreck somewhere between here and Harville.

She finally decided to hell with the first thing. If she was confident, she had nothing to worry about from other women, and she was, she ought to be confident she wouldn't be stood up. As for the second, she could do more good in town than she could out here. She picked up her bag and headed for the taxi stand.

She was so intent on her mission that she almost bumped into Ron without recognizing him.

"Janet!"

"Oh!" She dropped her bag, wrapped her arms around him, and gave him a kiss. During Janet's younger days, there had been a social taboo against PDA—public displays of affection. There had never been a social norm she was more delighted to smash. Affection was its own excuse; people who didn't want to see people engage in it were just jealous.

"Hi," Ron said.

"Yeah," Janet said. Her eyes gleamed behind her glasses. "Hi."

Ron bent over and picked up her suitcase. "Come on, we've got to go."

They practically ran across the parking lot to the rented car, a white Ford Taurus. Ron threw the suitcase in the back seat, opened the door for Janet (he remembered that sort of thing even in an emergency; he said his mother had been very insistent about it), then ran around the car and slid in behind the wheel.

"Ron—" she began.

"Sorry I was late," he said. "All hell is breaking loose."

"Oh? Something to do with your meeting this morning or something?"

"Or something," Ron echoed. "Only in a manner of speaking." He gave a bitter little chuckle. "It did have to do with security."

"What do you mean?"

"Clyde Pembroke's been kidnapped."

"My God."

"Yeah. It took practically an act of Congress to make the authorities let me come pick you up." Ron frowned. "You started to tell me something, didn't you?"

Janet gently patted his thigh. "It'll keep," she said.

The meeting had been called for eleven o'clock that morning; Chip Pembroke came by to pick up Ron in another Lincoln, not the same one Clyde had been driving the night before. Ron hopped in the front seat and buckled his seat belt.

"Isn't the Professor coming?" Chip asked.

"No," Ron said. "The Professor is painting."

"Oh, yes, he does that. I've read about that in *Parade* magazine. What is he painting now?"

"He is painting a picture of a mating pair of cardinal grosbeaks eating grapes. It's a very interesting painting, since, he tells me, it's hard to deal with red and purple together without making the picture garish. He's doing fine. It will probably be an extremely realistic painting—we're at that stage of things. It could go in a nature book, assuming cardinals eat grapes, which I don't know."

"Cardinal grosbeak? What's that?"

"That's the full name of the bird. You should know that, being the son of a devoted bird-watcher the way you are."

Chip grinned sheepishly. "That's Dad's hobby. He tried to get me interested in it, but it didn't work. You must know a lot about it."

"Not really. It just stuck in my mind because it sounded so perfect: Clarence Cardinal Grosbeak, Archbishop of Altoona."

Chip laughed. "I don't think there is an Archbishop of Altoona, but I get what you mean. Why didn't the Professor want to come along?"

"Because what we'll be doing today isn't philosophy; it's just nuts-and-bolts work. The kind of thing I do ninety percent of the time. He has no patience with it whatsoever. And, as he frequently says, no talent for it, either."

"That's a shame," Chip said. "Chief Viretsky was looking forward to meeting him."

"Gee, I suppose the chief'll just have to settle for a couple of multimillionaires."

"He sees them so often he's sick of them. You don't know what it means to be a Pembroke in this town."

"How could I?" Ron said. "My father sold insurance."

"Listen, Gentry," Chip said, suddenly serious. "Don't envy me, okay?"

"I don't, especially. I was just saying I couldn't know what it means to grow up the way you did."

Chip laughed. "Well, there's your first lesson. It makes you paranoid. It's also extremely isolating. I mean, it must be weird enough to grow up rich in New York, or even Pittsburgh, where there's 'society,' with dancing schools and that other crap for people at your income level. It's nauseating to think of—I've met plenty of dancing-class society in college and since—but at least it's somebody your parents don't have to warn you about.

"And, you know, my mother was worse than my father? She'd had all this wealth dumped on her like a Christmas present, and suddenly she was suspicious of the whole world, in case they would try to take it away from her."

They stopped for a red light. Chip drummed nervously on the steering wheel. "It was worse for me than it was for my dad and Uncle Clyde, you know. They were twins; they had each other. I didn't have anybody."

"You seem to have weathered it all pretty well," Ron commented. "You've got a successful business of your own."

Chip nodded and his face lit up a little. "*All* my own. I borrowed the money to start up Chip's Creamery Ice Cream from a *bank*. My dad was furious. You know, before I started this business, I made it through almost forty years of life and never had a *job*. I just sort of noodled along. Then, one day, I decided to take the thing I loved best in the world and just do it the best I could."

"And that was ice cream."

"Well, no, actually, that was playing shortstop in the major leagues, but I was already too old for that, so I thought I'd go to the ice cream next."

"I hear it's good stuff," Ron said.

"Thank you. I'm very proud of it. It's doing well, too. Of course, I'm never going to make Pembroke kind of money with it, but it keeps me off the streets. I'm about at the point where I can start using some profits to do some good. Like those two hippies up in Vermont. Brilliant publicity, and it doesn't cost them all that much. I think World Peace is pretty well played out as a cause, though. I think I'll go for the environment."

Ron said, "Ah."

"What's the matter?" Chip wanted to know.

"Don't do that until the Professor finds out what happened to the birds, okay?"

"Are you saying I could have chased the birds away with *ice cream*?"

"Of course not. I'm saying you can bet if there's something around to embarrass you, the press will latch onto it. I'm not talking about the local paper here—"

"Oh, naturally."

"I'm talking about the national media and the tabloid TV shows. Those guys will kill you if they get the chance. Did you see the one they did on the Professor?"

"Because he lives in your house? That one? Where it made it look like some kind of commune or something?"

"That's the one. I happen to own a twelve-room house— an old hunting lodge the city grew up around—and the Professor lives in three rooms on the top floor. To see that show, you'd think the three of us lived in a waterbed."

Chip shrugged. "See, there's something I wouldn't know about. Being famous, I mean. The Pembrokes have always managed to keep out of the public eye."

"Yeah, well, be prepared. When it gets out that Benedetti is down here, the press will be out in force, wondering where the serial murderer is."

They came to the entrance to the estate. The Lincoln rode a lot more smoothly on the pitted gravel road than Flo Ackerman's car had. Flo had been invited to today's meeting, but she'd declined. It wasn't her field, she said. She was going to hop a plane back to D.C. for the weekend and catch up on reports.

Ron was just as glad. He didn't look forward to another jouncing in that Mixmaster she called a car.

Their path through the estate took them past Omega House, into the woods and out back, into terra incognita for Ron. In about ten minutes, they reached an unassuming one-story cinder-block building, well hidden in the woods. From it, a paved road led out through the woods.

"Goes out to the highway," Chip explained when Ron asked about it. "Access for the milk trucks."

And, Ron thought, for such of Chip's employees who couldn't afford Lincolns. There were about ten cars in a small parking lot alongside the building.

"You've got people working on Saturday?"

"All the time," Chip said. "It's cheaper to keep the machines running."

Chip opened the door for Ron. The receptionist smiled, gave them a hello, and said, "Your father's here, Mr. Pembroke; he's waiting in the conference room. Chief Viretsky called—he'll be a little late."

"And Uncle Clyde should be along any time, now. Great.

We'll be waiting, Sandy. Send everybody right in as soon as they arrive."

Henry Pembroke looked tired and old this morning, more worn out than he'd looked fresh from the exercise machine the evening before. He kept rubbing the purple spot on his wrist.

Nevertheless, he struggled to his feet and shook hands with Ron. He nodded at his son, his face expressionless.

"Where's your car, Dad?"

Henry Pembroke shrugged. "The Mercedes is in the shop, and I just wasn't up to driving the Samurai. The thing will go anywhere, but on this terrain, the ride's too rough for an old man like me. I didn't want to go all the way out to the highway to come up the smooth road, either—I'd just get homogenized on the way out instead of the way in."

Unexpectedly, he grinned at Ron. "That's why my son had to pave the road, Gentry. If the milk trucks had to come in the regular way, he'd have to make butter instead of ice cream."

"What did you do, Dad, walk?"

"Yes, I did. Loved it. I should do it more often. There are still birds around here. I saw a cardinal on the way over."

"Was it eating grapes?" Ron asked.

"What?" Henry blinked. "No. Cardinals don't eat grapes. They're seed-eaters."

"Just wondering," Ron said.

He sniffed. The air was filled with a sweet smell, but it was much weaker than yesterday's, and it wasn't grapes. He sniffed some more.

"Butter pecan," he said.

"Close," said Chip. "Butter almond. With real butter and real almonds, as always. Real everything." He looked at his watch. "I wonder what's keeping Viretsky."

Henry Pembroke smiled, coughed, smiled again. "I know

what's keeping him. Cussedness. He just wants to make the Pembroke brothers wait to show us we don't intimidate him."

"Do you?" Ron asked.

"Intimidate Viretsky? No. And we never have. When he was a kid in this town, he was wild. Not bad, you know, just rambunctious, as my father used to say. Dropped out of school and came to work at the mill.

"One day, he got into an argument with a foreman over the best way to set up a grinding job. Called the foreman an idiot and worse, which he was, but you can't have that kind of insubordination on the shop floor. So Clyde called him into the office, and we told him we'd have to let him go."

Henry laughed under his breath. "And what he called us then! Said we could take our factory and do something uncomfortable with it. Said if what we wanted was somebody willing to kiss the ass of a fool, he didn't want to work there, either. He told us he'd make it—in this very town, without a bit of help from the great and powerful Pembroke brothers."

Henry sighed. "I always liked that boy. Anyway, he up and joined the army, finished high school there, went to college on the GI bill when he got out, joined the State Police, and took the chief's job here in Harville when it opened up three years ago."

"He's done a real good job, too," Chip said. "I used to know him a little. We're about the same age."

"The only thing that bothers Viretsky," Henry added, "is that Clyde and I supported his appointment to be chief. I don't think he'd be happy unless he was 'showing us' something, somehow."

The speaker on the small conference table buzzed. The receptionist announced the arrival of Chief Viretsky.

Ron was expecting a Mike Ditka type, a brawny, rebellious Pennsylvania Eastern European. Instead, the chief was small and slight. He'd been a Pennsylvania state trooper—if they had a height requirement, Chester Viretsky had just sneaked past it. He had thick, wet-looking black hair, and a bushy black mustache. Rimless glasses glinted on his thin nose.

Ron rose to shake his hand. The chief looked at him with little enthusiasm, but did manage a nod and a muttered "Pleased to meet you." At Henry's invitation, he took a seat. Despite his size, Viretsky moved with confidence, and the .357 magnum on his hip looked as if it belonged there.

"Where's Clyde?" he asked.

"We don't know," Chip said. "It's not like him to be late."

"Well, let's either get him here or get started without him. We've got seventeen thousand people in this town, and I work for all of them."

"We know that, Chief," Chip said. He rose. "I'll just phone Alpha House."

Viretsky nodded and turned to Henry. "You'll remember, Mr. Pembroke, that I urged you to get better security for this place when I first took the job as chief, didn't I?"

"Did you? I don't recall."

Viretsky turned to Ron. "You talked him into it, Gentry? How'd you do it? Fat consulting fee in it for you? How'd you get the brothers talking to each other again?"

"It's true I'm a PI, but I don't do a lot of security work. This is like a favor. Niccolo Benedetti is doing a job for the Pembrokes at the request of the Federal Government."

"Am I supposed to be impressed?" Viretsky demanded.

"No, Chief. You asked a few questions. I'm trying to give you the background so that the answers make sense, okay?"

Viretsky bent his mustache in a grin. "Don't be so touchy, Gentry. Maybe I am impressed a little. I've certainly heard of Benedetti. But doesn't he usually go after serial killers? I know the Pembrokes have their own way of doing things, but somehow I doubt they'd keep a series of murders from me."

Ron turned to his nominal employer. "Mr. Pembroke, I want to tell the chief what's been going on."

"By all means," Henry Pembroke said. He rubbed the purple spot on his wrist again. "I just wish I knew where Clyde is. If he's reneged on our agreement . . . Set me up to look like a fool . . ."

"Let's try not to jump to any conclusions just yet, Mr. Pembroke. Let me brief Chief Viretsky."

Ron went on to tell the chief about the missing birds, and about yesterday's dead cat.

When he finished, Viretsky was incredulous. "Birds? Cats? This has brought the World's Greatest Detective, so-called, to my town? It's *kids*, for God's sake. I never went so far as to smash a cat's head, but I knew plenty of kids who did worse things to them. It's wrong, and if I catch them, I'll kick their asses, but come on."

"What about the birds?" Ron said.

"What about them?"

"How do kids make a bunch of birds go away and stay away from one small area?"

"I don't know. Some kind of poison."

"Then there'd be dead birds, right? You ought to go take a look at the place. It's spooky."

"I haven't got time for that kind of foolishness. I'll leave it to the World's Greatest, okay? Now, we're supposed to be doing some kind of security plan, right, Mr. Pembroke? Until you and your brother can get a real consultant in here and put in a decent system? Then I think I'd better get started."

"I'll have Clyde's head for this!" Henry's face was brick red. "If my brother ever expects—"

He didn't finish the sentence. Chip came back in, frowning.

Ron was grateful for the interruption. Things were getting out of hand again.

"Uncle Clyde. He's not at home. His bed hasn't been slept in. He hasn't been to the factory. And his Lincoln is missing."

"And I take it he's not in the habit of taking nighttime drives in order to relax?"

"For God's sake, Gentry," Henry Pembroke said. "That's the stupidest thing I've ever heard in my life."

"Hang around me for a while," Ron suggested mildly. "What's stupid for one person is obvious for another. I hope you'll pardon me for saying so, Mr. Pembroke, but I've never seen two people for going off half-cocked like you and your brother. It's a wonder you weren't at each other's throats in the womb."

Viretsky smoothed his mustache, but not in time to hide a small smile.

"All I'm trying to say," Ron went on, "is that there's no reason to panic yet."

Just then, the receptionist bustled in with a white envelope. She handed it to Henry Pembroke, who sat there looking at it.

It bore no stamp or address. Just the words HENRY PEM-BROKE—URGENT printed somewhat sloppily in the unmistakably nondescript blue of a Bic Crystal pen.

"Put that on the table," the chief barked.

Henry Pembroke dropped the envelope as if it had burned him.

"Just leave it there," Viretsky said. "I've got to get some stuff from the car. Gentry, can I trust you to make sure nobody else touches that thing?"

Ron nodded. Viretsky disappeared. Chip looked stunned and hurt, like a man who's stepped on a stingray.

Sandy, the receptionist, started to babble. "It was delivered to your house, Mr. Pembroke, and your man, what's his name?"

"Mr. Jackson."

"Mr. Jackson went out to get the mail the way he always does, so he said, and he saw that in the mailbox with the regular mail, and it said 'Urgent,' so he brought it here, knowing I'd give it to you. But then I remembered Mr. Pembroke," she indicated Chip, "being so upset not being able to find his uncle. I thought, what if this is a message, you know? Like, what if it's important or something, and every second counts? Isn't somebody going to *open* it?"

"Chief Viretsky is going to open it," Ron told her. "It's got three sets of fingerprints on it already, at least. He's going to handle things so as not to smear up what's inside."

"Then you think it is . . . you know, important?"

"I think the chief doesn't want to take any chances. Now, Sandy, is it? Sandy. Good. You go back to your desk. The chief is going to want to hear your story firsthand—"

Ron cut himself off when he saw the growing excitement on Sandy's face.

"No," he said. "You just sit right here at the table with us, and wait for the chief."

Sandy sat down, delighted to be included in the big doings. No need to tell her that Ron had decided, if at all possible, to keep this young woman away from telephones until further notice. If this was going to hit the papers—and Ron was willing to guarantee it was going to hit the papers—let it happen in such a way that the chief couldn't blame Benedetti and Company for it.

A few seconds later, Viretsky came back inside, carrying a small valise. He was accompanied by a tall, thin black man dressed in natty light-blue sweats.

Henry Pembroke said, "Chief, is this really necessary? All Mr. Jackson did was deliver the letter."

"Don't worry about it, Mr. Pembroke," the tall man said. His voice made him sound a lot older than he looked. "Chief Viretsky explained why he wanted me here."

"Oh," Henry said, perturbed. "Perhaps Chief Viretsky'd be kind enough to explain it to me."

The chief looked at Ron. "Why don't you explain it to him, Gentry? I've got business to take care of. Please have a seat and relax, Mr. Jackson."

Viretsky looked around the table. He seemed to notice Sandy for the first time. "Why is she still here?" he demanded.

"I took the liberty of asking her to stay until you got back, Chief."

"You did, huh?"

"Yes, sir. I was thinking about when she phones her best friend about this, as she inevitably will, won't you, Sandy?"

"Well, sure," Sandy said. She didn't like the silence that followed, so she added quickly, "If I get permission, of course."

Ron smiled at the chief. "I just figured if she sat around, she'd have a much better story to tell—later. If she got permission. You're in charge, of course, and you'll decide what's best, but I wanted to make sure you had the chance to decide. For Sandy's sake."

The chief gave Ron a long, hard stare. Perhaps he was finding Ron hard to hate, and even partially useful. That was the idea, at least.

Viretsky transferred the look to Sandy.

"My men will be here any minute," he said. "Then we'll make different arrangements. In the meantime, enjoy. Gentry, go ahead and explain."

Viretsky opened the valise and took out a pair of white cotton gloves, a razor knife, and a tweezer.

Ron said, "The reason the chief brought Mr. Jackson back here, Mr. Pembroke, is that he handled the envelope. So did you and Sandy. You'll all have to be fingerprinted, for elimination. He'll probably have to track down the mailman, too, in case he touched the thing while he was putting the rest of the mail in the mailbox. Then, everything that isn't a fingerprint from one of the three of you or from the mailman might possibly belong to whoever put the envelope in there."

The chief had taken a little spray can from the valise, and was playing a fine black spray over the envelope. Lots of nice latent prints sprang to view.

Chip cleared his throat. He'd been so quiet Ron had almost forgotten about him. "This is an awfully big to-do, isn't it? Weren't you saying five minutes ago there was nothing to panic ourselves about?"

"The envelope wasn't here five minutes ago. There's still nothing conclusive. The chief is just smart enough to avoid taking chances."

"Don't butter me up, Gentry," the chief muttered under his breath.

Carefully, holding the envelope by its edges, Viretsky used the razor knife to slit it along the top. With the tweezers, he pulled the page inside free so that it sat, folded, on the table.

Viretsky held the single sheet of paper down with the tip of one gloved pinky against its edge. Using the tweezers, he pulled one corner until the top third was unfolded. He repeated the procedure with the bottom third.

The letter wasn't scrawled in ink the way the envelope had been. It was a careful cut-and-paste job, in the classic ransom-note style.

Ron could read upside down, even through a jumble of type styles and sizes. The note read:

PEMBROKE—

WE'VE GOT YOUR BROTHER. IT WILL COST YOU ONE MIL-
LION DOLLARS TO GET HIM BACK. INSTRUCTIONS WILL REACH
YOU. NO POLICE OR YOUR BROTHER DIES.

It wasn't signed.

"Or your brother dies." Henry Pembroke's voice was hollow.

"My God," Chip exclaimed. "What are we going to do?"

It occurred to Ron to suggest that it would probably be
okay to panic now, but he let it go.

T e n

Chester Viretsky heard the gasps and saw the shocked faces and reflected that the Pembrokes, in one way or another, had been giving him a pain in his ass his entire life. If it hadn't been the brothers lording over the town by virtue of their vast fortune or their very existence (or, most accurately, Viretsky supposed, by virtue of the very existence of their vast fortune), it was Henry's late wife, Sophie, prevailing upon his predecessor to fix the speeding tickets she got cruising around with her various boyfriends while Henry was out watching birds. Old Chief Supman had done it, too. Made Viretsky sick, and sick at himself that he hadn't reported it.

The only Pembroke Chet Viretsky had ever met who hadn't caused him trouble was Chip.

And he was starting in now.

"No police, Chet!" he yelled. "It says no police! Get out of here, quick, before somebody sees you!"

"Chip, you know I can't—"

"I know my uncle's in danger, for God's sake, and your being here with Dad could get him killed. Can't you understand that?"

Gentry was shaking his head. His dark eyes were sympathetic behind his big, square glasses, and he seemed to know what he was doing, more or less, but what the hell good was he? He was just another complication that Chet didn't need.

But, then, Gentry did something Viretsky could never have done. He touched Chip gently on the arm. At that point, if the chief had touched Chip Pembroke at all, it would have been to slug him in the jaw.

"Chip," Gentry said. "You're showing the family trait again; you're acting like a spoiled brat."

"The note says '*no police*'!"

"What if it said 'no gravity'? Chip, a two-year-old learns you can't make things unhappen. That bell is rung; you can't unring it. The chief knows, and the chief is going to do his job, and he's going to do his best to get your uncle back safely. Your smartest move is to help him do it."

Chip grumbled, then reluctantly subsided.

Viretsky took a deep breath. "Gentry's right. Even if I hadn't happened to be here, I hope to God you would have had the sense to call me. Now. The first thing we're going to do is play this low-key. Give me that phone."

Mr. Jackson was closest. He handed it across the table. The receptionist licked her lips as the phone went by, maybe because she was itching to blab, maybe because she was wishing for some popcorn. She was enjoying the show. She was going to have one hell of a story to tell.

The chief dialed headquarters and had them patch him through to the cars en route. "Forget it," he told them. "Go on with your regular patrol. I'll fill you in later. Yeah, yeah, ten-four."

Then Viretsky picked up the letter, still with the tweezers, put it and the envelope into the proper-sized evidence bags, and put the whole thing into the valise. "All right," he said. "I'll have to handle this myself, for now. No big police presence. Just go on about your business. But."

The chief snapped the valise shut. "Nobody says a word. Not one word. Not to a friend, a relative, an acquaintance, a fellow employee, nothing. Don't even write it in your diary until I say so."

Viretsky had been talking to the room at large, but he was staring directly at Sandy Jovanka, Chip's receptionist. She'd reddened a little when he'd mentioned the diary. She'd be safe enough through working hours, but afterward, the chief would have to think of some way to handle her.

"I want to stress what Mr. Chip Pembroke has said. His uncle's life is in danger, and a crowd of reporters around here can mess things up so badly we won't be able to get him back. If that happens, the person who shot off his—or *her*—mouth will, I promise, go to jail as an accessory after the fact."

He was glad there were no attorneys present to hear *that* one.

"We were supposed to make a security plan. If anybody asks, that's what we did, we made a security plan. If anybody asks what that is, tell them it isn't much security if everybody knows it."

Viretsky stroked his mustache.

"But if anybody—*anybody*—gets too curious, I want to hear about it, immediately. If anything happens, I want to hear about it, immediately. I've got a gimmick in my car that will record any calls coming in on a given phone. I'm going to stop at Omega House and install it there on the way out. Mr. Pembroke, Mr. Jackson, I suggest you get back there and make things look normal. Chip, you and Sandy stay here for the rest of the workday. You'll hear from—"

"I want to go back with Dad," Chip protested.

Viretsky took a breath. "Chip, you'll stay here with Miss Jovanka, okay? Keep up normal appearances, business as usual, that sort of thing. Can the two of you do that?"

Chip's face clouded. He was *about* to say to hell with business, it's my uncle we're talking about, and, besides, what do I care if she can do it, she's having the time of her life over this. Then the dawn broke. "Right, Chief," he said. "I've got it. Keep her busy. Quietly busy."

"Right." Viretsky nodded in the same exaggerated way. They must have looked like a couple of idiots, the chief thought. "I'll get back to you before quitting time. I'll get back to all of you long before that, as a matter of fact."

Henry Pembroke and Mr. Jackson were standing in the doorway. "It would be best if you got going now," the chief told them. "It wouldn't do for me to give you a lift."

He turned to Gentry. "You come with me. We're going to go talk to that professor of yours."

• • •

They rode in silence as far as Omega House. Ron watched as the chief carried the phone recorder, which he took from the trunk, into the house. Viretsky turned in a stellar performance as a man who had to go to the bathroom on the way in, and a better one as a man in an ecstasy of relief on the way out. Then the chief started the engine and jounced them out of there again.

"You did a pretty good job with them in there," Viretsky said. His tone sounded a little grudging, but it was sincere. "They might have gotten out of hand without you. Thanks."

"Glad to do it, Chief. Besides, a cop with the guts you have deserves support."

"What's that supposed to mean?"

"I mean, it was risky leaving them like that. I don't know what else you could have done, but I've known a lot of cops who wouldn't see that."

"What could I do?" the chief demanded. "You know it yourself, the security out there is a sieve. The Pembrokes have always been popular in this town, but being loved is no defense. I can't make a big show. Hell, if somebody saw me going out to the car for the fingerprint kit, Clyde Pembroke is already a dead man. I've got to regroup and handle this on the sly. God, I hope this isn't one of those cases that takes weeks."

"Me, too."

"Oh, Gentry, one more thing. I need your gun."

"Don't have one, Chief."

"Don't try this, Gentry, I'm warning you."

"I'm not trying anything, I promise you. I just don't happen to have a gun."

"Look, I'll overlook your not checking in with my department, which you are supposed to do when you hit town—at least as a courtesy. But if you keep jerking me around, I won't forget anything, understand?"

"Chief, I hate guns. I don't own one, never carry one, never fired one in my life."

"That's hard to believe."

"I know. I'm tempted to get one just so I don't have to go through this all the time. Look, I'm a licensed PI. I could get a carry permit in New York State easily, right?"

"Yeah."

"So check with Albany. They'll tell you I don't have a license at all."

"That wouldn't prove you didn't have a gun."

"Chief, do I really strike you as so stupid I would risk my entire career by doing without something I could easily get?"

Viretsky thought it over. Ron didn't find this especially flattering, but at least the chief came up with the right answer.

"No. You don't come across as stupid."

"All right, then."

"But I'm not sure I've got you figured out yet. You're a tough one to figure."

"People keep telling me that."

• • •

Ron opened the door to the suite and yelled, "*Maestro*, we've got company, and we've got a problem."

Benedetti came out of his room. Usually, he painted in his shirtsleeves, but he had the whole set of tweeds on now, complete with his bow tie. He was ready for action.

He bowed. "You must be Chief Viretsky," he said. "I am pleased to meet you. You have come to question me about the latest complications in the case."

"Who told you?"

"Mr. Henry Pembroke telephoned. His assumption was that since I was here at the behest of the Federal Government, I outranked you in this matter."

"Oh, yeah? What's your assumption?"

"My assumption is that for all their business expertise, the Pembroke brothers have been isolated by their wealth from even a whiff of reality, and concepts such as jurisdiction are alien to them. I, ah, educated him, shall we say. He will not question your authority again. Of course, if you will be so kind as to let me assist you in this matter, I'll be very grateful."

"I'll bet. What if I say no?"

Benedetti's face was too lean to look like a Manx cat's, but it was plenty feline all the same. "I will humbly obey."

"I'll bet," the chief said again. "Then, in twenty-four hours, the FBI comes in on the case, and you pull strings in Washington, and you're in and I have my nose pressed against the window. I haven't gotten *any* isolation from reality."

"It would be a disservice to all concerned to have a man of your perceptiveness pressing his nose to the window."

"Yeah. That's the way I feel, myself. All right, why don't you tell me what's really going on with the brothers, as long as we're working together."

"Ronald, haven't you filled him in?"

"Yes, *Maestro.*"

"He filled me with something," Viretsky said. "Am I supposed to believe this stuff about birds and cats? They'd really leave the rest of the United States choking bad air because of cats and birds?"

"Foolish behavior, *graz' Iddio*, is not my field, but it seems to me, human beings indulge in childish behavior until they are forced to stop." Benedetti shrugged. "Clyde and Henry have never been forced to stop. Therefore, they behave as children. Therefore, they don't weigh consequences. They just do what their wealth and whims allow them. Fortunately, they are a couple of benign specimens; this town is very like a dollhouse for them, and they try to make sure their toy is clean and well cared for."

"That's it!" Viretsky said. "That's exactly it! For years, these guys have gotten on my nerves, and you finally put the finger on why. We're like pets for them."

Benedetti raised a palm. "Try not to upset yourself. Many pets are badly treated."

"I suppose so, but it's galling." The chief shook his head as if to clear it. "Anyway, you can forget all that bird crap now, if you're going to help on the kidnapping."

"To the contrary. I agree that getting Clyde Pembroke back safely is the priority, if it can be done, but I have no intention of forgetting the incidents that brought me here. I am sure they are all part of a pattern."

"How can you possibly be sure of that, for God's sake?" the chief demanded.

Benedetti shrugged again. "Perhaps you are right. I am not logically convinced, but my intuition is strong. It is possible that after a peaceful and paternalistic lifetime, Clyde Pembroke might be kidnapped immediately after trouble with his brother over mysterious incidents concerning their primary boyish passions. I say it is possible; I simply do not believe it."

A quiet, high-pitched sound filled the air. "My beeper," the chief said. "May I use your phone?"

Benedetti gestured assent. The chief picked up the phone and dialed.

Ron looked at his watch. "Geez, I almost forgot. I've got to get out to the airport and pick up Janet."

"Who?"

"My wife."

"My other assistant."

Viretsky put the phone down and shook his head. "Not now. We're going places. The ransom instructions have come in."

E l e v e n

Harry Swantek was content with his life. He made more money than three previous generations of Swanteks combined. He had a house and a lawn and a gardener to take care of it. He was married to his high school sweetheart, and four kids later, he was still crazy about her. He had hunting in the winter and golf at Blind Ridge Country Club in the spring and summer. He had the respect of the community, and the feeling he'd earned it, having paid his way through college with a football scholarship to Pitt and summers working at the Pembroke plant.

The only thing he didn't like about the job was working Saturdays. Especially in the fall. Saturdays were for football. Specifically, high school football, the Harville High Welders, for whom Harry himself had starred at tackle twenty-one years ago. There was a magic to the crummy old concrete stadium as tough kids from tough towns fought to realize their dreams.

Home games weren't so bad, these days. The plant closed down at 1:00 P.M., kickoff time. Harry was usually able to get there by the middle of the second quarter. Games out of town, though, forget it. Perversely, Harry, Jr., a fullback, had his best games on the road.

Things would get even worse once the brothers got it all squared away and went into production on the smoke scrubber, Harry knew. The place would probably go into production seven days a week, and at least for the first couple of months, that meant Harry would have to be there. Harry Swantek took his responsibilities as vice president and plant and production manager very seriously.

Sometimes he wondered if the brothers, for all that he

owed them, felt the same way about things he did. Harry pushed the thought aside as unworthy.

He supposed Saturdays wouldn't be so bad if they weren't so damned boring. For the most part, the guys were happy to get the overtime, and were on their best behavior. Any problems that came up tended to be handled on the supervisor or, at worst, foreman level. All Harry had to do was sit around in his office, keep up-to-date on the technical material, and wait for the Big Emergency he hoped would never come up.

He was reading *Modern Industrialist* when his phone rang.

"Yeah."

"Mr. Swantek?"

"That's right."

"Murphy at the front gate. Federal Express guy just came. Dropped something off for you."

"On Saturday?"

"Yeah, they'll do that if you pay extra. Anyway, the thing's got 'extremely urgent' written all over it, so I thought I'd let you know."

"Sure, Murphy, I'll come down to collect it." He'd be glad to get a little air, anyway.

Harry went down to the gate, collected the package, and strolled back to his office, wondering. What the hell was it? It was just a little cardboard envelope, after all. Maybe a delivery contract or something, though he couldn't think of anything they had coming back, and he ought to know. There was nothing, at least, that merited this kind of urgency.

He sat at his desk and pulled the tab. Inside the envelope was a loose sheet of paper and a manila envelope. The loose sheet was addressed to him. Made up of letters cut from newspapers and magazines, it said:

SWANTEK:

> HERE ARE THE INSTRUCTIONS FOR HENRY TO GET HIS
> BROTHER BACK. SEE THAT HE GETS THEM RIGHT AWAY.

Harry had an idea that he knew what this all meant, and he knew it was nasty, but he also knew how to follow instructions. He called Omega House.

"Chip." Harry felt a little funny calling the son and nephew of the Pembroke twins by his first name, but Mr. Henry Pembroke had insisted on it, and it did seem a little dumb for Harry to be "mistering" someone younger than he was, whom he'd known (at least known of) virtually all his life, and who had nothing to do with Pembroke Industries outside of being a Pembroke. So Harry had gotten to the point where calling the younger Pembroke "Chip" felt natural. Almost.

"Get off the line, Harry," Chip said. "I can't explain now."

Harry heard fear in Chip's voice, and maybe concern, but there was also a large trace of the whine of a spoiled brat. Chip was expecting a call from someone, got Harry instead, and was upset about it. Chip might have been an okay guy if he hadn't been born with an entire silver service for twelve in his mouth. As it was, Harry could take him or leave him, but he'd rather leave him.

"I don't think you have to explain," Harry said. He read Chip the pasted-up letter.

"Oh, God," Chip said.

Harry asked, "Is this for real?"

Harry could almost feel the heat of Chip's hissed reply over the phone. "Of *course* this is for real, you jerk! Get over here right away with that information. And don't tell anybody!"

Harry controlled his temper. He always did. It was never easy, and the control didn't always last longer than the temper did, but he always tried, thanks to his freshman coach at Pittsburgh. After another fight during a hot practice, the coach pulled Harry aside. Instead of chewing him out, the man said, "Son, if you don't learn to control your temper, it's going to control *you*."

So things that used to get him boiling now only bubbled him a little. What bothered Harry were the times he let go. His temper didn't get out as often these days, but it was bigger. And meaner.

"Look, Chip," he said. "I know we have our differences, but I'm with you and your family all the way on this. I want you to believe it."

For ten seconds, nothing but a soft hiss came over the phone, and Harry could feel himself losing it again.

Finally, Chip said, "I do believe you. Just tense. Get over here right away, all right?"

"Sure thing," Harry said. He grabbed the manila envelope, still unopened, and went.

• • •

On his way out of the hotel room with the Professor, Ron was buzzed by the front desk, who told him the rental car he'd ordered had arrived, and the guy had some papers he wanted him to sign.

"Okay," Ron said. "I'll be down in a minute." He turned to the Professor. "Well, there's a detail I forgot. It's nice to know that when I finally get to pick up Janet, I'll have a car to do it in."

"Yeah," Viretsky said. "You'll even have it with you."

"What do you mean?"

"I mean, we're taking your car. Let's go."

Ron shrugged. Downstairs, the guy from the auto rental place got his signature, checked him out on the car, and off they went.

"We're going to stop at headquarters first," the chief told them. "I've got to do a couple of things. Won't take long."

One of the things, Ron assumed, was getting the lab started on the kidnap note and envelope. He hoped whatever else the chief had in mind would be as brief as promised. Janet was a woman of almost infinite virtues, but extreme patience was not among them.

As expected, when they got to headquarters, an old-fashioned brick-and-whitewashed-wood building with glass globes alongside the front steps, the chief first stopped at the lab, then led Ron and the Professor to his office.

"Wait here," he said, then disappeared into another room. Ron could have sworn that as the chief went through the door, he was already whipping off his tie and glasses like George Reeves on the old *Superman* show.

He was gone ten minutes. Ron spent seven of them drumming his fingers on the desktop.

"*Basta, amico,*" Benedetti said at last.

"What the hell is he doing?" Ron demanded. "The ransom note is sitting there, and he's probably got the football game on now, to see if Notre Dame is covering the point spread."

"I doubt it, *amico,*" the Professor said. "I find Chief Viretsky an interesting man. His only flaw is a pride too easily bruised. He has to do things his own way, but I believe he gets satisfactory results."

"I don't consider a fight with my wife, which is impending, to be a satisfactory result."

"Don't exaggerate, Ronald. Janet may be worried, but she won't be angry. Perhaps you can phone the airport and leave a message for her."

"That's a thought. The chief didn't say anything about our not using the phones, did he?"

Ron picked up and dialed information without waiting for an answer. Then he got the airport, learned that Janet's

flight was due any minute, left a message that he'd been de-
layed, and sat back relieved. A little.

Ron looked at the old man, who was grinning happily to
himself. He hated it when Ron drummed his fingers.

Ron was just about to start doing it again when Viretsky
returned. At least, he thought it was Viretsky. The mustache
and the glasses were gone, as was the grease from the hair,
which was now two shades lighter and parted in the middle.
The uniform had been replaced with a suit of some soft material in tan, with a dark-aqua shirt and a purple tie. He
looked like an English teacher at a private girls' school.

"Chief?" Ron said.

Viretsky smiled. He looked fifteen years younger than he
had before.

"Halloween isn't for another month and a half," Ron informed him.

"Yeah? Well, who's to say which getup is the costume?"
Even the voice was different, slightly softer, less tense.

"I see," Benedetti said. "The first note said no police—"

"Right. So I'm giving them no police. In case they're really watching. And I'll be on the scene if that's the way things
work out. Now let's go to Omega House."

"I'm not sure I know how to get there."

"I'll give you directions."

• • •

Chief Viretsky, whatever he looked like now, was still very
much the efficient cop. He had his valise with him, his razor
knife, and his gloves and his tweezers, and he removed the
contents of the manila envelope with the same care he had
used before.

The message began, "Henry Pembroke."

"Typewritten this time," the chief said sardonically. "We
can *try* to trace this." He looked carefully at the Pembrokes,

father and son, as he said this, so Ron figured he had said it for psychological effect.

That had to be the only reason he'd said it. Electric and electronic typewriters, let alone word processors and printers, had made typewritten evidence useless years ago. The electric motor meant there was no longer any eccentricity to a typist's style. All keystrokes hit with the same weight. As for idiosyncrasies of the typewriter itself, all a kidnapper had to do was throw the daisy wheel and the ribbon cartridge in the furnace or the river, and no one would ever be able to trace the thing. Ron had a sneaking suspicion their kidnapper knew this.

Ron looked over the chief's shoulder. The next word was "Tonight."

"Tonight?" Ron said. "What's with this guy?"

"It doesn't matter," Henry said. "I'm just glad this isn't going to be a drawn-out thing."

"Nevertheless," the Professor said. "It seems to be an optimistic expectation that anyone could raise a million dollars in cash—I assume they want cash."

Viretsky looked at a later sheet. "Yep," he said. "In used tens, twenties, and fifties."

"We can pay it," Henry said. His voice was soft but determined.

"How, Dad?" Chip demanded. "We don't keep that kind of money around the house."

"No, but we've got it in the bank."

"Well," Ron said. "You're not going to get it from a cash machine in the side of the wall. Do you have enough pull with the owner of the bank to get him to open up for you to make a million-dollar withdrawal?"

"Clyde is the president of the bank." Henry sounded almost smug.

"Oh," Ron said.

"I am the vice president. In Clyde's absence, I'll authorize the transaction myself. We have accessible accounts in that bank that will yield the right amount of money."

"Wait a minute," the chief protested. "How do you know for sure they've got your brother? How do you know he's still alive?"

Henry shook his head in resigned impatience.

"We're twins, Chief. We grew from the same cell. He's a part of me. I'd know if he weren't alive."

"Mystical nonsense," Benedetti objected amiably. "The operational question is more to the point. Do you, Mr. Pembroke, care to take the chance that the kidnappers *don't* have your brother, and ignore this note?"

"Of course not. What do you take me for, Benedetti?"

The old man shrugged. "Some things need to be put on the record, that's all. I meant no offense."

"I'll pay. Don't you interfere, Viretsky. I mean to pay this money and get my brother back, and God help you if you try to stop me." The way he was leaning forward, head thrust out and small fists clenched, made it look as though he wouldn't mind working off some of his pent-up anxiety on the person of the chief.

"Wouldn't dream of it, Mr. Pembroke," Viretsky said. Ron could detect no trace of sarcasm. "Getting the victim back safe is always the top priority."

"What are the instructions?" Benedetti asked. "Where is the money to be left?"

"Doesn't say. It's one of those goddam paper-chase deals. They want Henry Pembroke, or his representative, to drive east on Dropham Road—that's the one that parallels the front of the estate here—and he'll be signaled what to do next."

Henry Pembroke looked suddenly old. Ron thought he could see purplish lines in the man's face now, he'd turned so pale. "I . . . I don't see too well at night, now. What if I miss something?"

"You won't miss anything, Dad," Chip told him. "I'll be with you."

"Uh-uh," Viretsky said. "Too risky. Look what it says here: more than one person in the car; any sign of cops; any sign of a gun; any sign anyone is following you—Clyde Pembroke dies instantly."

"Oh, my God," the victim's brother moaned.

"I'll go alone, then," Chip said. His voice had wavered on the *o* of alone. He tried again. "I'll go alone. I'll deliver the money."

"No," Ron said. "I'll do it."

Benedetti shook his head. "A brave suggestion, *amico*, but not an intelligent one. You cannot go."

"Why not?"

"Think."

Ron thought about it, saw what the Professor was driving at, and felt like an idiot.

"I'm sorry, *Maestro*."

"You have still to learn not to let your impulse toward heroism get in your way."

Viretsky furrowed his brow. "Why the hell can't he go?"

"Because Ronald has no idea of what instructions are to be given. If he receives a message that says to go to the abandoned cottage above the old reservoir, or some other esoteric local landmark, how is he to know where the reservoir *is*? He needed your directions to find this place, if you'll recall. Ronald has excellent qualities, but he cannot become an expert on local geography in less than a day."

Viretsky tried to work his way out of sending Chip. Ron knew he was worried about losing a second Pembroke in search of the first, and Ron didn't blame him. It was something he'd been thinking about, too.

But what could be done? Send one of Viretsky's men? Any sign of a cop, Clyde dies instantly. And this was obviously a snatcher, or group of snatchers, with a lot of local expertise.

They might know the cops by sight. They may or may not have been able to recognize the new-look Viretsky, but the chief couldn't take that chance and he knew it. They didn't dare put Ron in the car with an expert on local geography because the kidnappers, who seemed to be on top of things, specifically forbade more than one person in the car.

"How about a radio link?" Chip suggested. Then his face fell. "Nah," he began.

Viretsky looked sour. "Yeah. They might give him time limits to get from point to point. If he's got to radio back the directions he gets, and wait for an answer, he'll blow it."

"I'll go," Chip said.

"Furthermore," Ron added, "they could easily intercept a radio transmission."

"I said, I'll go."

Ron figured Chip, like anybody in this situation, was holding on to his courage by his fingernails. He didn't need people trying to convince him to drop it. "Wait a minute," he said. "A cellular phone. It would be hard for them to tap that."

"It is possible, however, *amico*. Remember the embarrassment to the House of Windsor," Benedetti said.

"Yeah. The Princess of Wales thing. But the guy who intercepted that phone call had special equipment."

"As might the kidnappers."

"Besides," Chip said, "you're famous. Sort of. Anyway, your picture has been in the paper with Professor Benedetti's as a famous crime fighter. They might recognize you, too, and get scared. When they see me, they know they have nothing to worry about."

"It'll be dangerous," Viretsky said.

"I think I know that," Chip said. He swallowed.

"You must take some precautions," Benedetti told him softly. "I have a few ideas."

T w e l v e

The sign said HARVILLE, EXIT ONLY, 1 MILE.

Janet said, "Where was Sandy during all this?"

Ron took his eyes off the road for a second to look at her. Janet wished he wouldn't do that.

"Sandy? The receptionist? I tell you a tale of missing birds and brutalized cats and kidnapping and courage, and you want to know about a bubbleheaded and blabbermouthed receptionist with a yen for the telephone?"

"I've got other questions," Janet said primly. There was a time when an outburst like that from Ron would have upset her for a week, but she'd learned about his sense of humor—and the tense times, the times during which he was most likely to indulge it. "I just like people to be accounted for," she said. "For that matter, what about Mr. Jackson?"

"He was attending to his duties. That guy has more duties than an army platoon. Sandy was upstairs more or less locked into a guest room with the telephone removed. Whenever she complained, Chip kept reminding her that she had never punched out from Chip's Creamery, and was currently earning time and a half, soon to be double time, for lying around on a bed reading magazines. She said she wanted to talk to him about a bill from Northeast Flavors and Fragrances that she couldn't understand, but he told her it could wait. Probably forever."

"What were the precautions the Professor was talking about?"

"Ah, wouldn't you like to know?"

"Yes, I would."

"Well, me too. Seems the Professor is getting coy on us, saving the precautions until just before departure time."

"Which is?"

"Nine o'clock sharp. However this turns out, we probably won't have to stay up too late. Have I told you that I love you and I missed you, and I don't want to spend four nights in a row away from you anymore?"

Janet smiled inwardly. Take that, Flo Ackerman. "Not for the last ten minutes or so."

"I love you," Ron said, "and I missed you, and I don't want to spend four nights in a row away from you anymore. Also, I wish I was doing the goddam errand tonight."

"I don't," Janet said.

"That's all well and good, but I've got a hell of a lot better chance to make something worthwhile out of this than Chip does. Although he did show some guts, today. The thing is, he hasn't— I'm glad you're here."

"You said that."

"I mean it professionally, this time. We could use some psychological expertise."

"I'm at your service, darling. Professionally and otherwise."

Ron's grin lasted only a second. "Keep a close eye on these people. I haven't had a chance to talk to the Professor yet, but I got an itchy feeling about this."

"What do you mean?"

"The kidnappers are almost too smart. God knows they're too goddam *confident* for me."

"What do you mean?"

"The ransom instructions. They were delivered to the factory, remember? Viretsky ran it down. It was a legitimate Federal Express delivery. It had been picked up from a Federal Express drop box at a mall outside Scranton at five-thirty Friday afternoon—yesterday.

"So at five-thirty yesterday afternoon, Benedetti, Flo Ackerman—and where the Professor got this stupid idea I'm interested in her is beyond me—"

"Shhh," Janet said. "He never said you were interested in her, he said she was interested in you. She'd have to be crazy not to be. Go on."

"At five-thirty yesterday afternoon, we were beating our way through silent and odd-smelling woods. The dead cat had yet to be found. The brothers hadn't confronted each other over it yet. I hadn't had my bright idea about beefing up security. Clyde hadn't gotten in his car to head home."

Janet nodded. "I see where this is going."

"Yeah. The kidnappers are so sure of themselves, they arranged for the delivery of detailed ransom instructions *before the snatch ever took place.*"

T h i r t e e n

Flo Ackerman was back, and she was angry.

"Why wasn't I told about this?" she demanded.

"Because it didn't have anything to do with you," Chief Viretsky told her. "And because I didn't want this news spread all over Washington, D.C., while there's still a chance of getting the victim back."

"I can keep a secret as well as anybody!"

"Sure you can," Viretsky said. "Everybody in D.C. can, when they feel like it. Unfortunately, they've usually got some reporter they'd rather keep buttered up instead, so they don't."

"You—"

Viretsky showed her a hand, like a traffic cop. "If you happen to be among the one-tenth of one percent who don't go running off to the press when they think they can get an edge from it, then I apologize. *If.*"

"And it does too have to do with me," Flo insisted. "I've worked for months to bring the two together, to get that device into production. This could ruin everything."

Benedetti said, "Excuse me, Miss Ackerman, but could it also not save everything?"

Flo said, "What?"

"From your point of view. I speak only hypothetically, but please, be, as Huxley advised, humble before the facts."

"I don't know what you're talking about."

"*Peccato.* I will try to be clearer. The problem, from your point of view, is that the brothers are estranged, and that Henry was blocking the project out of pure animosity toward Clyde. You were unable to budge them from that position.

Now observe. Clyde is missing, and Henry is visibly distraught, even now drawing one million dollars, *buon'Iddio*, from the bank to pay ransom.

"If Clyde is returned safely, surely his ordeal and the generosity of his brother will bring them back together in this project that will profit them greatly, and be of great benefit for the human race."

Viretsky touched his face with his right hand. He did it twice, trying to adjust the glasses and smooth the mustache he no longer had.

"Professor," he demanded, "are you trying to say that *she* had something to do with this?"

"All I am trying to do," Benedetti said, "is to imagine. That is the whole of what I can bring to these endeavors—imagination and humility. I imagine, and check the fruits of my fantasy against the known facts, then imagine again, always—humbly—ready for correction or additional knowledge. Until I have imagined a story confirmed by real observations and events."

"But—" the chief began.

"I am only in my first imaginings, Chief.

"Still, it may be instructive for me to continue. Look again. What happens if Clyde Pembroke does not return safely? Then Henry becomes the sole authority on what is to happen at the plant. Would he not see the continuance of the project as a tribute to his brother? Would it not be simpler to deal with one brother instead of two?"

Flo looked at the two men. The chief's face was coolly appraising; Benedetti's wore a catlike smile that gave away nothing. Were these two going to charge her with a kidnapping she knew next to nothing about? They seemed ready to charge her with a murder that, for all anybody knew, hadn't happened and might never happen.

This was not the way she'd planned things when she

picked up the phone early that afternoon, just to check how Gentry's little security meeting had gone. She'd gotten an obviously frightened Jackson telling her everything was just fine, couldn't be better, you bet.

And she started to worry. A lot of her future career was tied up in this. She tried the call again. This time, Jackson, who was obviously getting cues from someone else, kept telling her, no, ma'am, Mr. Henry Pembroke couldn't come to the phone, and, no, ma'am, everything was just fine, and he was ever so sorry, but he had to clear the line for a very important call, and, yes, ma'am, he'd tell Mr. Henry Pembroke she'd called.

And he'd hung up on her.

That was the weirdest thing of all. She'd been dealing with Jackson for some time now, and he had to be a contender for the title of Politest Living Human. There was nothing subservient about it—the man was just genuinely nice. For him to hang up the phone without saying goodbye was as good as a scream from someone else. Something was wrong, and they were keeping the news from her.

What the hell. She'd planned to go back to Harville tomorrow, anyway. She canceled her date (a producer with ABC news—if Flo had anything to do with it, Chief Viretsky would never know how close he'd come), hopped in her car, and drove north and west.

Well, she'd found out what was wrong. She just hoped they weren't trying to frame her for it.

"I . . . I think I'd better call my lawyer," she now told the chief.

Viretsky looked surprised. "Do you know a Pennsylvania lawyer? You need to make a statement or something?"

"Chief," Benedetti interjected, "I believe I have frightened her. I am so sorry, Miss Ackerman. I was only trying to show you why the chief is right to be cautious. Not only with you, but with all of us."

"Including you," Viretsky told the Professor.

"Of course, you must include me. I have no apparent motive; indeed, I should enjoy breathing clean air as much as Miss Ackerman would enjoy providing me with it. But motives can be hidden. So inquire, by all means."

He turned to Flo. "At that, Miss Ackerman, Niccolo Benedetti is not so blind as to see the inconsistency of his own imaginings. For if you were indeed sufficiently calculating to plan the kidnapping or murder of one of the Pembroke brothers to make a million dollars or to speed your career, or both, you would also be able to calculate that Henry Pembroke would have been an infinitely better target."

"Why—" Flo's voice seemed rusty. She cleared her throat and tried again. "Why do you say that?"

"Because if you—or your confederate . . . That is why no one will avoid suspicion in this case—alibis mean nothing. One can buy a good amount of conscience-free help with the promise of considerably less than a million dollars. Where was I? Oh, yes. If you or a confederate of yours wound up killing a kidnapped Henry Pembroke through design or inadvertence, the survivor would be Clyde, who already desires to produce the smoke scrubber."

"I still think maybe I need a lawyer."

Chief Viretsky got impatient. "No, you don't. Not only are you not an active suspect, you aren't even being questioned. The Professor's questions were all . . . what do you call it?"

"Rhetorical."

"Yeah, rhetorical. He didn't even wait for answers. You're here now; you drove a couple hundred miles and barged in. You're welcome to stay until we work this out. Whether you have the run of the place—within reason—or wind up locked in one of the extra rooms is totally up to you, Miss Ackerman. Okay?"

"That's not much of a choice, Chief."

"It's the only one I got. No. You could also be brought to the station. I can hold you for forty-eight hours. This thing should be over for better or worse by tonight. Plenty of time for me."

Flo looked at him. She had met the chief briefly a time or two during her numerous stays in Harville, and she'd thought him a typical small-town geek. With the grease out of his hair, and the glasses and the mustache gone, he'd be presentable anywhere. But why she thought a change in appearance would bring a change in small-town, power-drunk attitudes, she didn't know.

So she was stuck. Be a good girl, or spend the night in jail. She'd be good. Flo didn't want to admit it, even to herself, but she'd be glad to efface herself for a while. Benedetti had scared the hell out of her.

Gravel crunched on the driveway.

"They're back," the chief said. "Here's your chance to see a million dollars in one lump, Miss Ackerman. Unless, of course, you've ever been to lunch with a congressman and a lobbyist." He smiled as he said it, though, and headed for the door.

Flo tried to think of anything else to do besides follow him. She couldn't. Before she could get started, though, Professor Benedetti laid a hand on her arm.

"Miss Ackerman," he said. "It wouldn't be prudent to allow your imagination to run free, as I did mine, in the presence of the Pembrokes. There is no need to mention any possibility of failure in tonight's exchange of prisoner and ransom, eh?"

She looked at him. "Professor, have I angered you in some way? I'm not in the habit of gratuitously hurting people."

"No? Well, I have been known to do it, despite my best intentions. Please forgive me if I hurt your feelings."

"You got me pretty upset," she began. But, she realized, she didn't want to fight Benedetti. She didn't even know what kind of ammunition would affect him. She told him it was all forgotten, and moved toward the hallway.

The chief was just opening the door, but it wasn't the Pembrokes, father and son. It was Ron Gentry and his wife, Janet.

Flo needed this like a hole in the head.

• • •

"Oh," Viretsky said as he opened the door. "It's you."

Janet tried to imagine how the chief had looked "greased up," as Ron put it. She supposed she could, but she couldn't imagine why she'd want to. His voice and body language said here was a self-confident man having the confidence tested, and doing his best not to show the strain.

"Golly, Chief," Ron said. "I'm overwhelmed to see you, too. This is my wife, Dr. Janet Higgins. Chief Viretsky."

Janet held out her hand and the chief shook it.

"You'd better come in," he said grudgingly.

He led them though a maze of modernity to some kind of sitting room. Flo Ackerman was there, looking angry and scared; right now, more scared than angry. Janet had planned exactly how she was going to handle this. She ran to her old friend and hugged her warmly.

"Flo," she said. "I've missed you."

Flo, her face muffled somewhere against the much-taller Janet's shoulder, said, "Me, too." Janet took her by the shoulders and held her at arm's length.

"You look great! Even better than last time!"

Flo looked at her. Finally, she said, "So do you." But it wasn't the usual girlish gush. The observation seemed compounded of equal parts sincerity, wonder, and resentment, and it was one of the most soul-satisfying things Janet had ever heard in her life.

"Perhaps," Benedetti said, "you and Miss Ackerman can catch up with old times later. Right now, I need to brief you and Ronald on the most recent events. Sit down, please."

Janet shed her coat and sat, thinking, You and Ronald, *ha*. Benedetti had never openly resented Janet's presence in Ron's life, or in his cases, for that matter. In fact, he frequently complimented her on her intelligence, and said what a pity it was he hadn't been able to train her when she was younger. But he had never, not once, ever given her or anybody else reason to think that in his eyes, she was Ron's equal in assisting him. Until now. He even put her first. She knew it was a mind game he was playing with Flo (Janet wondered what else the old man had done to Flo), but she would treasure the memory nonetheless.

"The chief has had his men pursuing a number of angles while you have been gone, Ronald. Chief?"

The chief had to chew it a few times before he let it out. Apparently, he had decided the best thing to do was to cooperate with Benedetti in the manner to which the Professor had become accustomed, but he obviously didn't like it.

Still, Janet could see that having made the decision, the chief was going to stick with it.

"Mostly negatives," Viretsky said at last. "I checked discreetly with Harrisburg and with local FBI. They have no knowledge of any known bad guys arriving in the vicinity lately. Not this kind of bad guy, anyway. Federal Express has been checked out—that computer they talk about in the commercials really works. This thing was dropped off at their box in the South Scranton Mall some time between noon and five-thirty yesterday. Payment was included in cash."

"Is that usual?" Ron asked.

"Not unusual. Anyway, it was the exact amount for a Saturday delivery, which is a little more than Monday through Friday."

"Well, that makes sense," Flo said.

"I think what the chief is driving at," Ron said, "is that whoever is behind this either knew or took the trouble to find out a lot of little stuff. He knew this guy Swantek would be at the plant on Saturday to get the message. What about him, anyway?"

Viretsky shrugged. "Solid citizen. Plant manager for the Pembrokes, vice president of the corporation. Local guy. I've known him all my life. Special protégé of Clyde's. Sort of like the son he never had, you know?"

"Does he need money?"

"Now, how the hell am I supposed to answer that? Do these Wall Street guys, who've made five hundred million dollars legit, then start scams, need money? Did that movie executive who forged signatures on checks need money? I've seen enough thieves to know that only a tiny minority of criminals steal because they need money. The rest of them just have a bug up their ass."

Benedetti nodded solemnly. "Excellent, Chief," he said. "Crudely put, perhaps, but accurate and profound. It is the attempt to understand the origin and nature of that 'bug' that constitutes my lifework."

"Yeah," the chief muttered. "Good luck."

"Philosophy aside, Swantek's one of the few people outside the family circle and the people here who know about the kidnapping," Ron said. "So what about him?"

"He's been spoken to, and told to keep his mouth shut. Also, he's being watched, and knows it. I've got good men on him. Happy now, Gentry?"

"Sure. Just making certain. But I was making a point, wasn't I? What the hell was it?"

"Things the kidnapper knew or found out," Janet reminded him.

"Right. Thanks. He knew about Swantek. He knew Henry could get a million dollars out of the bank on Saturday afternoon, a trick not many of us could pull off. He knew he could slip the other note, the one Jackson found, into the mailbox without being seen."

"Well, Gentry, the thing is out there on a public road, for crying out loud."

"Okay, scratch that one. Try this one. He knew or guessed or found out that Mr. Jackson would be likely to pick up that letter and get it to Henry before Federal Express delivered the follow-up."

"He might," Viretsky objected, "have just dumped the thing in there. Clyde would still be kidnapped. The ransom demand would still get there. What's the difference?"

"Big difference," Ron said. Viretsky glared.

"I agree with my young colleague," the Professor said. "A crime of this sort is a drama, scripted by the kidnapper. He must draw his own shadowy character with care for the benefit of the other unwilling actors in the play.

"He must convince the family of the victim that he is indeed desperate enough and cruel enough to murder the person who has been kidnapped if the ransom demand is not met. At the same time, he must present sufficient rationality to inspire the belief that the victim will, in fact, be released unharmed if the ransom is paid.

"Most importantly, he must project an air of *competence*. He is the dramatist, he is (or needs to be seen as) the god of this particular universe. Dr. Higgins?"

When Janet was a child, it had been a schoolyard game for boys to sneak up on each other, or on the girls, and throw them something, anything from a red-pebbled kickball to a wadded-up tissue, yelling, *"Think fast!"*

The first few times Benedetti had interrupted his pontifications and called on her without notice, her first instinct had been to respond the way she had in the playground—throw her hands in front of her face and scream.

She hadn't (though she had let loose with an unladylike "Huh?" a couple of times), but it had made her uncomfortable enough to ask the Professor to stop. He had refused, sweetly, telling her that eventually her confidence in herself would equal the confidence he had in her, and then she wouldn't mind it.

Well, she was still waiting for the confidence to click in, and she still minded it—a little. But she had learned to expect to be pushed into the spotlight at any time, and she was rarely, if ever, caught at a loss.

And she had begun to be flattered by it, too.

"The Professor is right," she said, reflecting that that was always a safe opening. "Kidnapping, like so many other violent crimes, has at least as much to do with the perpetrator's desire for a sense of power as it does with a desire for money. The victim, or victims—the loved ones of the person kidnapped are as much the targets of the crime as the actual kidnappee—are almost always financially successful, and frequently famous, at least on a local or regional basis. The kidnapper may have a specific grudge against the victim-family. Or he may simply be bitter at his own insignificance."

Everyone's eyes were on her. Janet cleared her throat. "I say 'his.' Kidnapping for ransom is almost exclusively a male crime. There are frequently women accomplices, but a lone woman, or a group of women, kidnapping someone for ransom is virtually unknown."

"That stands to reason," Viretsky said. "Thank you, Dr. Higgins."

"I'm sorry it's not much help. After I've seen the notes, and know more about the whole situation, I might be able to narrow down the profile from 'unhappy male' for you. If you'd like me to, that is."

"Sure, go ahead. We don't have any shortage of unhappy males—I'm one of them—at the moment. And even if you can't do anything else with the profile, it'll be a pleasure to tell the FBI when they get here that I've heard it already."

"Look at the bright side," Flo said. "Maybe you'll get it all settled tonight. Maybe you'll catch them. Then you won't need the FBI."

"Maybe," Viretsky said. He didn't sound confident.

Heavy doors opened. "I think," the Professor said, "that Henry and Chip have returned."

F o u r t e e n

Chip Pembroke could feel his eyes glazing over, as if being coated with a silver spray for the purpose of showing him movies projected from inside his head. He was really about to do it. He was really about to leave the safety of Omega House and drive out into a misty fall Pennsylvania night into the teeth of a crime.

Well, he'd gone too far to turn back now. Uncle Clyde was out there, waiting for him. Chip had no choice but to go. The script was all written; the actors were in their places. All Chip had to do was finish out his part.

Just that.

He was getting a last-second briefing. Three of them, actually. One each from Professor Benedetti, Chief Viretsky, and Ron Gentry. Details varied, but the burden of the songs was consistent. Don't be a hero.

"Look," Viretsky said. "Follow directions. Do whatever they tell you. If they put a blindfold on, don't peek, okay? If they want the suitcase, let them take it. Just try to remember."

"Remember what, Chief?" Chip was having enough trouble remembering his own name at this point.

"Everything you can remember," Viretsky told him. "Sights, sounds, smells. Anything that might help us pick up the track, later."

"Right. Maybe I can—"

"Don't do anything extra. Just follow instructions. Now, you're going to take the Samurai, right?"

Chip frowned. "I was going to take my father's Lincoln."

Viretsky shook his head. "Don't. Take the little car instead."

"Uncle Clyde would be awfully cramped in the Samurai, especially if he's . . . not in such good shape."

"Don't worry about that; we'll get him an ambulance even if he's only tired. The point is, your uncle's car is also missing; it may come into the case, one way or another, and have to be traced—tire tracks and so on. There's no sense in taking the chance of crowding up the crime scene with a virtually identical car."

Chip thought about it for a few seconds.

"Okay?" the chief demanded impatiently.

"Huh?" Chip said. "Oh, sure. Now that you've explained it, I mean. What's a few extra bumps?"

"Good boy," Viretsky said. He turned to the Professor. "You got anything?"

"Yes, the precaution I spoke of earlier. You will keep in touch with us. The chief agrees."

Chip looked at the chief. He looked sour, as if he didn't like it, but he nodded.

"Isn't that kind of risky?"

"I will be frank with you, Mr. Pembroke. This is a move for your own protection. A person capable of kidnapping is capable of anything. If you stay in touch with us, we are much more likely to be able to come to your aid if you should need it. You will use a simple cellular phone, and your call will come right through to the house here, where the chief controls the situation. I am assured that while it is a simple matter to intercept and monitor police calls, it takes quite sophisticated technology to intercept a satellite-relayed telephone call." The old man opened his palms. "That is, if you are willing to use it."

Chip tried a shaky grin. "Willing? I was going to insist on it. I've thought of this myself, you know. I may not be a genius like you, Professor, but it's my butt that's going to be on the line tonight."

"Precisely. I think this is very wise of you."

"I've got a few conditions, though."

Benedetti raised an eyebrow. Chip could see this old man was not used to other people's setting conditions for him. Too bad, he thought.

"First, this 'staying in touch' stuff is to be strictly a one-way operation. Don't talk to me, because I won't answer. If I can do it, I'm going to put the earpiece of the phone out of commission. Also, I am going to explain—frequently—why I'm talking away on the phone, that I'm doing it for my own safety, period."

Benedetti nodded with his lower lip stuck out. "In case anyone *does* contrive to listen in. *Va bene.* A sensible precaution. I approve."

"Finally, if I scream for help, come running!"

"It's a promise," Ron Gentry said. He was the only one who wasn't smiling.

"Look," Gentry said. "What you're doing here takes a lot of guts."

"Thanks."

"You have a right to be impressed with yourself."

"Believe me, I'm not."

"It can happen. I know. This bravery is dangerous stuff, and a little bit goes a long way."

"I'm not sure what you're talking about, Ron."

"You do something brave, so when the opportunity presents itself, you push the envelope a little. Then a little more. The next thing you know, you're taking chances that don't help anybody."

Chip shook his head. "You're talking to the wrong guy."

Ron took off his glasses and polished them on his tie. "I'm not so sure," he said.

"I am."

"Okay. Just remember two things."

"Gee, the chief wants me to remember everything."

Gentry's smile was half indulgent, half impatient, as though he knew Chip was resorting to humor to keep his spirits up.

"Remember these starting now. One, the only thing that matters is getting you and your uncle back safe, and, two, all the kidnappers want is the money. It's in their best interests to keep violence to a minimum. Yours, too."

"Okay, Ron. Thanks."

Gentry stuck out his hand in a gesture of what Chip was sure was genuine friendship.

He would have been touched, but right now he had other things on his mind.

"Time to go," Chip said. He started for the door.

"Wait a second," Gentry said.

Chip felt his heart stop. "What's wrong?"

"Don't forget the money."

Chip let out a sound between a laugh and a wheeze, but inside he was kicking himself. He must be more nervous than he thought.

"No, I'd better not forget that, right?"

"I wouldn't have let you forget," Viretsky said. "One of my men is bringing the car around. Another one will bring the suitcase to the car."

The chief had insinuated three of his men into the house in the plausible guise of bank guards accompanying the million in cash from the bank to Omega House. Chip was just as glad to have them there.

"Right," he said again, and once more headed for the door. He could hear the high whine of the small four-wheel-drive vehicle he was to be driving grind to a stop. The cop/bank guard put the suitcase behind the seat. The cellular phone was there already.

"The number's already in there," said the cop who relinquished the driver's seat to him. "Just push redial when you're ready."

"Yeah," Chip said. He couldn't believe he was really about to do this. He slipped in behind the wheel. It was a little hard to breathe. "Thanks."

Viretsky, Benedetti, and Gentry all had last-minute instructions. Chip heard them, but they didn't register. It didn't matter anyway, they all boiled down to the same thing: *Don't be a hero.*

Chip Pembroke put the car in gear and drove off down the bumpy road wishing he could have reassured them.

He didn't have the slightest intention of being a hero.

F i f t e e n

Lights flashed; tape hissed quietly through the recorder attached to the phone at Omega House.

Everyone in the house had been gathered into the parlor—with only three cops and Ron to help him, Chief Viretsky decided it would be easier to keep an eye on everyone if they stayed in one place.

They sat in silence, leaning in toward the speakers like a Depression-era family listening to FDR on the Stromberg-Carlson. The chief sat with his eyes closed, trying to visualize what was going on. Benedetti had his head tilted to one side, like a man at a concert trying to ascertain if one of the flutes is a little off. Flo Ackerman gnawed her lower lip. Sandy Jovanka, Chip's receptionist, had a puzzled look on her face like a kid who hadn't expected a math test.

Henry Pembroke and Jackson, the housekeeper, sat together on a love seat. It was hard to tell who looked more nervous and miserable, or who was closer to tears.

Ron and Janet knelt by the big kidney-shaped coffee table, tracing Chip's reported route over the (to them) unfamiliar territory on a large-scale map of Harville provided by the chief.

Not that there was much to listen to, just the low hum of the motor, and the occasional terse report by Chip that he'd gone another ten miles on the road the kidnappers had chosen.

He'd just made the second such report when the chief sighed. "They're not going to contact him."

"But they left the instructions," Flo protested.

"Dry run," Viretsky said, shaking his head. "They just want to make sure we're willing to dance to their tune."

"It also," Janet said, "increases the uncertainty of the family, and their desire to get it over with."

Henry Pembroke's voice was hoarse. "I can't take much more of this. I . . . I'm not a well man."

"You must be strong," Benedetti told him. "Whatever happens."

"How?" Pembroke demanded. "My twin brother and my son are in God knows what kind of danger, and . . . and the chief says the kidnappers are probably just *toying* with me, and you tell me to be strong. How am I supposed to do it? Where is this strength supposed to come from?"

"Mr. Pembroke," Benedetti said, "if there were a formula for that, a technique for finding strength in oneself, what a better world this would be, eh?" He showed a little smile. "In your case, I can only offer suggestions. Would you care to hear them?"

Pembroke said, "Anything." Ron noticed that Jackson nodded, too.

"Very well," the Professor said. "I suggest you use your anger."

"My anger?"

"Of course. Your brother, and through him, you, have been the victims of a cowardly and sadistic act. Now your son is in peril—I would call it moderate danger, but even that is too much—because of his desire to help. Surely, your fury must equal your fear. Hold on to it. Cherish it. Promise to devote your life and fortune to tracking down whoever did this, however it turns out. Look forward to the day when *you* will be calling the shots, and the kidnappers will live in fear of you."

"They will, too, damn it," Henry said. His angry gaze went right past them, into the future, where it was designed to fry the perpetrator with just his eyes.

"I am glad to hear it. Later times may call for different responses, but for now, hold on to your anger. I remember—"

But the Professor never got to tell the story. Chip's voice burst from the speakers. "There's something! Chief, somebody in black popped out of the woods. He's got a sign. It says, 'PEMBROKE, STOP HERE.' I'm stopping."

"Be careful," his father intoned to the air. Whether he remembered that in deference to Chip's wishes, the chief hadn't hooked up the sending apparatus for this phone or not wasn't clear.

The motor came to a stop. A heavy car door opened and closed. Minutes of silence.

Then the door opened and closed again, and Chip's voice came back, breathless.

"Okay. I didn't get a good look at him. He was all covered up, scarf or ski mask or something, and he wore a hat. I thought of chasing him, but like you all said, I'm no hero. There was a note on a twig about five yards in from the road. It says 'PUNCHY'S PHONE BOOTH COIN RETURN SLOT. NO COPS. BE ALONE.' Says I've got five minutes. I think I can make it."

"He can make it," Viretsky said. "Even in what he's driving. Gentry, Punchy's was a roadhouse on Route Sixty-three, about two miles past the junction of Route Six."

Ron made marks on the map. "I've got it," he said. "I can see why they'd want to use a place like a roadhouse—it's crowded and easy to keep Chip under surveillance. But the coin slot seems a little amateurish. What if somebody uses the phone in the meantime? Sixty-eight point seven percent of the people in this country check the coin return after they make a phone call. Anybody can find that note."

Sandy spoke up. Of all people. "No," she said. "The phone booth is in the parking lot, the one he must be talking about. Because you couldn't get to the one inside. Punchy's burned down about three months ago. I saw the flames. My girl-friend Wanda and I were heading out there, you know, we didn't know what was going on, and then we saw the lights from the fire trucks, and the flames in the sky, and one of the state troopers told us to go back. Lucky nobody was hurt. It said in the papers later it was a grease fire, but I think it was the *mob*. You know, the M-A-F-I-A. Because there was a lot of gambling going on at Punchy's, football slips and like that, and the mob wanted their cut. I don't want to tell the chief his job, because I certainly wouldn't want him telling me how to file an invoice, but I bet the mob is behind this, too. They want the money they can't get from Punchy's now that they burned it down. That's why I think Mr. Pembroke shouldn't worry too much. The mob are terrible people, and all that, but if they get their money, they're happy."

She fluffed her hair and sat back again. "At least, that's what I think."

A little silence followed.

"Well," the Professor said pleasantly. "Now we know what you did all day locked up in that little room."

"I was thinking," Sandy said. "I think a lot."

"A rare pastime in these sorry days. We are grateful to you."

"It was bubbling in me," she told him. "I had to let it out or explode."

"Explosions are so messy," the Professor agreed, and Sandy subsided, pleased with herself.

Ron was pretty pleased with himself, too. Just look at what Sandy had managed to spin out of the fact that she'd once driven in the relative direction of a grease fire. If he'd given her access to a phone earlier, she could have produced a whopper that would put Burger King to shame.

Anyway, it passed the time.

Chip's voice snapped from the loudspeaker. "Okay, here I

am." Again, the in-and-out with the car door. "They're send-ing me to a hollow tree one point six miles up Route Six. That's got to be another note."

And so it went, for a good hour, reports from hollow trees and mailboxes to abandoned houses, jumping Chip around, but never letting him get far away.

"They must know by now he's not being followed," Pem-broke said irritably.

"They set the paper chase up in advance, Mr. Pembroke," the chief told him impassively. "Nothing to do but play it out."

Ron studied at the route he'd traced out on the map. It made a sort of ragged red rectangle, punctuated by stars where Chip had made his stops.

"Look at this," he said quietly to Janet. "See this big square in the middle?"

"Yes."

"This is us. This is the Pembroke estate. I think—*Maestro*," he said, raising his voice slightly, "I'm beginning to get a hunch."

"I'm sure you are, *amico*. I can see your pattern from here. Most interesting."

"But if I'm right?"

"If you are right, what are we to do about it now? Without adding to the danger?"

"What are you talking about?" Viretsky demanded.

"Show him, *amico*."

Ron handed over the map; the chief looked at it.

"I'll be a son of a bitch," he said.

"What are you talking about?" Henry Pembroke demand-ed. He was practically shrieking. "I insist on knowing what you're talking about!"

Before they could answer (or refuse to: Ron never knew how the Professor would react to a situation like this), the loudspeaker broke into the conversation.

It was Chip, and he was excited.

"They're sending me back to the estate!" the voice said. "To the old main gate, around back. I'm supposed to leave the money in the old gatehouse and pick up a note."

"Bet I know what that last note says," Ron offered.

"Sure," Viretsky said. "It's simple now."

Henry Pembroke was trembling with rage. "Not to me, goddammit! What are you talking about?"

"Your brother is somewhere on the estate," Ron told him. "Wanna go surprise them?" he asked the chief.

"Want to? You bet your ass. But we're not going to do it—too much risk."

"You're probably right."

"You know damned well I'm right. The nerve of the bastards."

"We can at least get ready."

That they did. Ron helped the professor into his coat and reached for his own. Janet was getting ready to go out as well.

"You stay here," he said.

"Ron, I love you, but never say that to me again."

"Oops."

"'Oops' is right. Tell me if you think something is dangerous. I have no desire to rush into danger for no reason. But something's bothering me tonight, and I think I ought to be in at the end."

"All right."

"Do you think it *is* going to be too dangerous?"

"Probably not," Ron conceded.

"Then I'm going."

"I love you even when you push my nose in," he told her. "I must be sick."

"Me, too. I love you even when it deserves to be pushed."

Viretsky horned in. "Can we break this up before the kiss, please?"

Chip's voice blasted from the loudspeaker. "I've dropped off the money. The last note says Uncle Clyde is in the old barn. I'm heading there now!"

Viretsky turned to Henry Pembroke and snapped, "How do we get to this old barn?"

"I'll show you," Pembroke said. He tried to get up but his legs didn't work. His eyes looked glassy.

Mr. Jackson bounced to his feet. "I'll show them, Mr. Pembroke." He grabbed a jacket from the coatrack. "Come along, gentlemen," he said. "I understand there's no time to waste."

Jackson and Benedetti were both old, and both about the same age, but they were the first to clamber into the chief's car in front of Omega House. Viretsky hopped in, put the red light on top, and was reaching for the siren.

"I don't think that will be necessary, Chief," Benedetti said. "I doubt there will be much traffic to clear away on the way."

"Good point."

Viretsky didn't drive any slower for lack of the siren, however. The car sped from one poorly maintained, narrow road after another as they made it through the thick woods. He and his passengers were tossed around like peas in a bladder. Janet held on to Ron for dear life.

"Turn—turn here," Jackson said. It was a nightmare ride, with branches reaching like skeletal fingers into the headlight beams, and the shifting mist taking on the shapes of ghosts.

Then they came to a clearing. There was a big barn, weathered gray with time and neglect, looking lonely for the now-destroyed house it had been built to go with.

The white Samurai nearby looked incongruous next to the massive old structure. The door of the vehicle stood open, and in its headlights, they could see Chip running across the lawn.

It didn't seem possible, but the chief drove even faster across the clearing. Ron was sure he was going to flip the car; he was half-convinced Viretsky wanted to take the thing airborne and fly the rest of the way.

Despite the speed, it seemed to take forever to get there. Finally, the chief spun his wheels to a stop about ten feet from the Samurai.

Ron opened the car door just in time to hear a scream.

He froze, as did the chief.

Ron looked at his wife, and said quietly. "That sounded like Chip. I think there may be danger, now. Would you consent to kindly stay in the car, please?"

"I will. But—"

"You, too, Professor."

"Prudence would dictate so."

"You, too, Gentry," Viretsky said. "You're no cop. And I know you don't have a gun."

"Well—" Ron began.

But the chief cut him off. "No arguments."

"I wasn't going to argue. I was going to tell you I would, but that I am moving to the driver's seat, in case anybody has to go anywhere in a hurry."

"Good thinking. You know how to work the radio?"

"Yeah."

"Call headquarters, tell them I want all available units."

"Be careful, Chief."

"Yeah." He pulled his gun and went toward the barn, sticking to the shadows.

Ron made the call, persuaded the dispatcher he really was talking for the chief, and that the chief really did want all available units.

Then he turned to the Professor. "I hate this."

"A man who liked it would not be normal," the Professor told him. "What has happened to Mr. Jackson?"

Janet was talking earnestly to the old man, making him follow her finger with his eyes, shining her pencil flash into them to see pupil reactions.

"He bumped his head during the last rush," Janet said. "He's a little woozy. I want to make sure he doesn't have a concussion."

"Well, hang on to his head if we have to take off out of here. I probably won't be any gentler than the chief."

"I hope Mr. Pembroke is all right," Jackson murmured.

"Here is Chief Viretsky now," Benedetti said, and there he was. Waving his arm in a beckoning motion, Viretsky gestured for them to come.

Ron got there first. "What is it?" he asked.

"A mess. I wanted your wife, but I knew I couldn't get her without the rest of you, could I?"

"I doubt it."

"Yeah. So I'm going to do something incredibly stupid and let the three of you go in there."

"Without you?"

"Yeah, without me. I'm going to stay out here with Jackson. He's a nice old man, and I don't want him to see this."

"Bad?"

"Weird. Also, Chip— Ah, I'd rather let you see for yourself."

"All right."

The Professor and Janet had joined Ron. He told them what the chief had said.

"*Andiamo*," said the Professor.

"Don't touch anything," said the chief.

The small door on the side of the building was creaky on its hinges, but it opened readily enough. Ron pulled it open and went in.

He'd been ready for a scene of gore and carnage, but there wasn't any. What was there was possibly worse.

The barn was one huge room, illuminated by a single kerosene lamp set on a bucket in the corner. It cast monstrous shadows on the walls and ceiling.

In almost the exact center of the room, Chip Pembroke knelt on a dirt floor, drawing abstract figures in the soil with his fingers. His face was blank. He seemed to be drooling a little.

Janet crowded in behind Ron. "Do you hear a baby crying?"

"Sort of," Ron said. He pointed.

About ten feet from were Chip knelt, Clyde Pembroke sat, tied to a chair. Even at this distance, it was easy to see he was dead. He'd been strangled; the old piece of rope was still around his neck. His face was nearly black, and his swollen tongue stuck out of his mouth. His clothes were twisted as if he'd struggled frequently and unsuccessfully with his bonds. His gray head was thrown back.

On his forehead, mewing pitifully, sat a small, red Manx kitten.

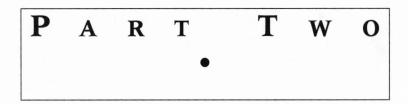

PART TWO

·

O n e

Ron Gentry rolled over in his sleep, and sixteen needle-sharp claws dug into his shoulder.

"Auggh," he said.

Beside him, Janet woke up and asked in a sleepy voice what the matter was.

"Will you kindly disengage this creature from my flesh? Why the hell does it have to pick on me?"

"It likes you," Janet said, gently and not too quickly removing paws from her husband. "He likes you. You're warm."

"Yeah, that's my best quality, my body heat. I don't mind his sleeping on me so much, it's his refusal to go along with it when I move. Besides which, you're going to get us thrown out of the inn with this thing."

Ron didn't really believe that. He thought he'd learned all about his wife's passions in the years they'd been married, but he'd never suspected her passionate desire to own a cat. Since she'd first laid eyes on this one, she'd somehow beguiled Chief Viretsky into letting her "look after the cat," bribed the maid at the hotel, spent a hundred bucks on various cat stuff, including a special cat bed the critter never used, and vamped Ron into going along with it all.

They'd even named it, too, for its tendency to pounce on things, like shoes, with or without feet inside, and attempt to eat them. He was Nimrod, mighty hunter.

He was also, Ron hastened to admit, a welcome distraction from the gloom of the past couple of days. Today was Clyde Pembroke's funeral. It had been decided that the least they could do for the poor bastard was hang around for the funeral.

It had not been, Ron reflected, one of their triumphs.

Viretsky's cops, rushing to the scene, had found nothing and noticed no one on their way. The barn yielded no clues. The body told nothing except that the murder had occurred somewhere between a half-hour and forty-five minutes before they'd seen Chip run into the barn.

It made an intriguing little mystery.

"I don't get it," Ron had said. He, Janet, Professor Benedetti, and Chief Viretsky were sitting in the chief's office downtown as they awaited autopsy results. Now they'd come, and they made things worse than ever.

"I don't get it," he said again. "Chip followed every instruction to the letter; he was literally on his way with the money, and *then* they decided they're going to waste Clyde Pembroke. It doesn't make sense."

"Maybe they decided he'd be too big a threat if they let him live," Janet suggested.

"I'd buy that, if they killed him sooner. The way they did it, it almost made things more dangerous. A little heavier foot on the gas pedal, and Chip might have walked in on them right when they were tying the knot."

Viretsky grunted. "Lucky for him they didn't. They probably would have done him, too."

"How is he?" Janet asked.

"Shook up, but fine. Apparently, his shock wore off even before they got him to the hospital. They'll hold him overnight for observation, but nobody seems to be worried."

"There is one thing we have to worry about," Benedetti said. His voice surprised them. He had been sitting back in the office's one armchair with his eyes closed; they had supposed he was asleep. Ron told himself he should have known better—the old man missed nothing.

"What is that, *Maestro*?"

"The fact that whoever did this thing is still out there."

"*Maestro*, I suspect they're halfway to Brazil by now. If I had just taken hold of a suitcase with a hot million in it, I wouldn't let any grass grow under me. And I'd want to get on the other side of any potential roadblocks, too."

"They don't have any million," Viretsky said. He turned to the Professor. "Didn't you tell them?"

"You seemed sufficiently put out that your man mentioned it in front of me. I assumed you would share the information in due time."

Viretsky gave a kind of puzzled shrug, then turned back to Ron. "They don't have any million," he said again.

"Funny money in the suitcase? That was a pretty big chance to take with Clyde's life, wasn't it? I mean, at the time, nobody knew what the setup was supposed to be."

"The money in the suitcase was fine. They just didn't take it."

"What?" Janet said.

"They didn't take it. Never touched it, as far as we can figure. One of my men found it in what's left of the old stone guardhouse, at the old entrance to the estate that was used when Humbert One lived in the main house."

"Which is now gone," Ron said.

"Right."

"But the barn is still there."

"You know it is," the chief said. "You were in it."

"And the old guardhouse is still there."

"What are you driving at, Gentry?"

"And the *money* was still there. A million bucks."

"That's what I've been trying to tell you. I don't suppose this is the time to tell Henry Pembroke, but at least he has the consolation of knowing that it didn't cost him a million dollars to get his brother back dead."

"That doesn't make any *sense*." Ron was so confused he was angry.

"Sure it does," the chief told him. "Before, he had a million bucks and a brother. He might have had no million bucks and no brother. Instead, he's got no brother, but he hangs on to the million bucks."

"That wasn't," Ron informed him, "what I was talking about."

"I know," the chief told him, "but what you were talking about is going to keep me awake nights as it is, without having my nose rubbed in it."

"As a favor to me, Chief Viretsky, let Ronald go on. I believe sleep will be difficult for all of us."

Ron could see Janet shudder. She was probably thinking about the scene in the barn. She sometimes said she had too much empathy to do this kind of work. She stroked the cat again as if the action soothed her.

The chief shrugged assent. "All right. They plot this thing out in detail, to the point of learning the Saturday routine at the factory. They had so much confidence, they sent their ransom note *before* they made the snatch.

"Then, Friday night, right on the grounds, they kidnap Clyde in his own car—that *was* his car you found out in back of the barn, right?"

"That was the one. Clean as a whistle, too. These guys are good at cleaning up after themselves."

"Any trace of a fourth car?"

"Fourth car?"

"Yeah. Yours, Chip's, Clyde's, and the car they must have gotten away in. Any oil drips or tire tracks?"

"Not on gravel," the chief said. "They could have had a Rolls-Royce or a pogo stick, for all the lab can tell. The only way we can prove they were ever there is because they left a dead body behind. It's what we call circumstantial evidence."

"Figures. Sometimes you wonder what makes them so lucky," Ron said.

"It runs out," Benedetti said. "Luck of any kind always runs out."

"I hope you're right, *Maestro*."

The Professor looked at his protégé. "I am not in the habit," he said, "of being wrong."

If Ron had said anything to that it would have been either a lie or a boost for the Professor's ego, which needed a boost like a porcupine needs a pin cushion, so he skipped it.

"To continue," Ron said. "They kidnap Clyde in his car. Somehow they winkle him out of his house.... No. They pick him up outside the cattery, right? That's where he got the cat. He'd been on the way there when he found the dead cat in the first place, and that distracted him. So he went back to the cattery to get that one."

The green-eyed kitten looked up from Janet's lap.

The chief raised his hands. "Of course. He had it with him when he was snatched. I've been going crazy trying to figure out some Satanic message or God knows what in leaving a cat on the corpse. The cat was there because he was with Clyde, that's all."

Janet frowned. "Well, he certainly was hungry when we got here, Chief. He drank most of the milk in the refrigerator. Not that there was much."

Janet rubbed the red fur under the chin, and the kitten let loose an audible purr. "I don't understand why Clyde would be there at night taking a cat away, though."

"He might have been on his way to give it to somebody," Ron suggested. He told his wife how Clyde Pembroke made a practice of giving away the kittens he wouldn't keep for breeding.

"See," he explained, "that one's a stumpie. Couldn't show him. Probably was planning to give him away to someone.

"All right. So the kidnappers pick up Clyde outside the cattery, and then they have the unmitigated *gall* to hide him on his own estate. They plant a note that's supposed to be found ahead of, or simultaneously with, the one with the ransom instructions.

"One of them actually exposes himself to danger to get Chip's attention for the first of the paper-chase notes—by the way, did Chip keep them?"

Viretsky nodded, lips tight. "Not that they're worth a damn. Lab is working on them, but they tell me not to expect much."

"What about that sign?"

"What sign?"

"The one that told Chip to stop in the first place."

"Oh. I've had men out looking for it. No luck yet."

"So Chip's doing everything they want. He goes up hill, down dale, and all around the estate—his path I traced on the map looked like an electron cloud, with the estate as the nucleus—he actually *drops off the money.*

"But what have our playmates done in the meantime? They've decided, 'Oh, to hell with it. Let's just *murder* the poor bastard and forget the money, what do you say?'"

Ron slapped the chief's desk. "I do not believe it. I simply do not believe it."

The chief shrugged. Ron noticed he was doing a lot of that lately.

"I wouldn't believe it, either. But we've got the body. And we've got the dough. I'm just a cop; that's all I know now. The question I want to ask is, what the hell can I do about it?"

Benedetti roused himself enough to light a cigar, a twisted, black, evil-looking thing. He took a drag on it, then said, "The cat."

"The cat?" Ron and the chief spoke simultaneously; they

turned to look at the kitten in Janet's lap, who returned their stare and raised them a meow.

"I do not refer to the animal itself. Although undoubtedly an eyewitness to the crime, I do not think it will be easy to get his testimony."

He stood and walked over to Janet, stroking the kitten with one lean brown finger. "I refer to the circumstances of the kidnapping as we have imagined them. The trip to the cattery. For whom was Clyde Pemberton choosing this kitten, eh? I should like to know that. I should like to know everything about it. Perhaps it was not coincidence, but a part of the plan."

"You mean, *Maestro*, that they used a request for a kitten to finger Clyde?"

"It presents itself. The enemy tries to exploit the weakness. How many people have told us Clyde Pembroke cherished a weakness for cats?"

"Okay" the chief said, "I'll find out who worked at the cattery. Or they'll find me. There'll be no keeping this quiet. I'm going to turn that Sandy loose, I guess. Then I'll track down Clyde's cat people."

"My associates and I should like to talk to them as well." The Professor was gracious. "After you have finished with them, of course, Mr. Viretsky."

"Yeah," Ron said. "It will give us an opportunity to return the kitten."

His wife shot him a dirty look.

"This cat is property of the estate," Ron told her. "And evidence, for all we know. The only reason the chief let you take him was that nobody else had the time or the inclination to take care of him."

"Well, he's sweet," Janet said.

And that had been the moment Ron had known he was doomed to be a cat owner. Or, more accurately, owned by a cat.

Sunday was a quiet day; the only thing on the agenda was the professor's trip to the cattery.

On the way there, jouncing yet again on a rutted gravel road, Ron decided that if he were ever rich, he'd either have a fleet of luxury cars, or, more sensibly, *pave* all the goddam roads on the estate.

The cattery was a long, low rectangle of cinder block—it reminded Ron of a bunker in a war movie—clean, neat, and loud, with various cats—all red Manxes with tails of various lengths—making an astonishing variety of noises. It was like walking into a jungle.

"Nimrod's relatives," Ron said.

Janet, who was suddenly having trouble controlling a cat who hissed at every other of his kind he caught sight of, said, "Looks like a dysfunctional family."

The attendant's name was Fred. He was in his sixties, had unruly salt-and-pepper hair, and wore wire-frame glasses, through which they could see weepy eyes of a beautiful blue.

He didn't know, Fred said, who Mr. Pembroke would have been giving the kitten to, though he was a bonny one, wasn't he? No, nobody else would know, either, he was sure. Mr. Pembroke often came by at night to make sure everything was all right, or just to spend time with his cats.

"I don't know what's gonna become of them, now. This is such a nice cattery. Well run. I don't suppose the other Mr. Pembroke will want to keep it going, him and his *birds*. Blamed nonsense that a bunch of cats in cages can scare off birds a couple of miles away. I don't know, maybe Mr. Swantek will work something out. Mr. Pembroke thought an awful lot of Mr. Swantek, thought Mr. Swantek was never much for cats."

They thanked Fred for his time, and tried to return the kitten.

"Oh, no, no," Fred said. "I see how it's taking on with the

other cats. Happens sometimes when they've been away from their mothers, you know. If he were show material, he'd be worth coaxing out of it, but as you can see, he's a stumpie, and, besides, his ears don't sit quite right." He lowered his glasses and leaned forward. "Tell you something else," he said. "*I* won't feel quite right around this cat, him being with Mr. Pembroke when, when—"

"Okay," Janet said quickly. "What do we do with him?"

"Keep him. At least for now. I guess he belongs to the estate, you know, but that won't be settled for a while. It's not like the cat was worth anything. . . ."

And that was where it had been left. They'd gone back to the inn, for two more days of waiting before the funeral.

Things got strange.

For one thing, the Professor just flat out disappeared. He retreated to his room, smoking and painting, taking his meals from room service and never calling for Ron even once.

Ron wondered what the hell the old man could be painting, since one way or another, the job was done, and the smoke scrubber would go into production, tra-la, and everybody but Clyde Pembroke would have the benefit of it.

For another thing, Janet was acting weird. She'd get mad over the strangest things, then five minutes later tell him he was the most wonderful man in the world. She positively doted on the cat, and seemed to take it personally when he was less than crazy about the thing.

And, of course, the cat just loved Ron to bits. It sat on his morning paper and purred at him. It climbed into his breakfast and purred at him. It killed his shoes and purred at him. It gave his trouser cuffs a nice coating of red cat hairs and purred at him.

Monday night, when Janet went out with Flo Ackerman (she'd told Ron not to worry, there'd be no bloodshed), Nim-

142 • William L. DeAndrea

rod had made Ron his own private gymnasium, climbing him like K2 before finally deciding to settle down on his lap.

Actually, it wasn't so bad when the little fur ball just sat there warm and fuzzy and purred.

Then Janet had come home and they'd gone to bed and made love, and Nimrod showed he had enough sense not to interrupt *that*, then he climbed in with them, and nestled down on Ron, and dug in his claws every time Ron moved.

And Tuesday morning was the funeral.

T w o

Harry Swantek was crying so much he couldn't knot his tie; Emily had to do it for him. Harry couldn't do much of anything over the weekend. Couldn't see. His eyes were always filled with these goddam tears.

Harry had always thought of himself as a tough guy. Not in the bar fighter sense, but in the sense of being able to deal with anything that came up. Now he was facing the fact that that wasn't true.

Emily was understanding, but the kids were scared, staying clear of Harry as though afraid to make matters worse. He'd stayed in a locked office at the factory all day yesterday, fielding condolences to the company from vendors and customers and competitors. Personally, he didn't feel very condoled.

Harry had always known what a big part Mr. Pembroke had played in his life, how he'd helped his ma with money so Harry could go to college instead of work, how he'd hired him and trained him and put him in his current position at the factory. But he hadn't realized how much he'd loved the guy. He hadn't cried this much since his own father had died, and he'd been twelve then. Harry wished he'd done a better job of letting Mr. Pembroke know how much he appreciated it all.

He also never realized how easily he could be scared, or how thoroughly. As a kid, he'd never backed down from a fight, no matter how big or how tough the other guy was. He gave his lumps, or took them, with the same stoic valor that was part of the world he grew up in. As a man, he'd steered clear of bars and other supermacho venues where men's grips on their tempers slipped with the lubrication of alcohol. Harry had too much to lose to risk blowing it in a fistfight, but he'd learned that in business you had to be just as tough, and just as resilient. He'd taken a few hits when he was learning the ropes, and he'd learned. He hadn't cried, and he hadn't run.

Now, though, he cried so constantly he embarrassed himself, and his legs were twitching with the urge to get out of town. Harry had to face it, he was scared. Not just the fear you overcome, the fear that's the measure of courage, but real, deep-down gut fear, the kind that turns your mind to mush and your knees to jelly.

Yesterday morning, trying to console him, Emily had said, "Well, honey, Clyde Pembroke left at least part of the company in good hands. You're going to do him proud."

The fear had rushed over him like a polluted wave, freeing his long-caged anger. He jumped to his feet, roaring, knocking over the table. His big hands were fists, and he was flailing them.

Harry thanked God that he still had enough humanity left not to have hit his wife—he would have killed her. Instead, he took his anger out on *things*, things he'd bought with the money earned as a Pembroke employee. He smashed the table, then used the table leg to demolish a couple of interior doors.

He screamed at his wife. *"Don't you say that! Don't you dare say that in front of anybody! Do you want me to go to jail for the rest of my life?"*

God bless Emily. She might be a little plump, and have some gray in her thick brown hair, but she was still twice the woman any other female in this town was. She was scared—who wouldn't be?—suddenly closeted with a maniac like that, but she stood her ground, and asked him what he thought he was doing. "All I said was—"

"You as much as said we ought to be happy Clyde is dead because of the block of stock he promised to leave me!"

Emily shook her head, speechless.

"The police call that a *motive*, Emily. I could be accused of killing a man who saved me from a life in the mills—"

"Oh, bull," Emily spat. "You sell yourself short, Harry Swantek, and I want you to stop. You weren't *handed* this, you know. You earned it. You prospered, but only because you helped the Pembrokes prosper, and don't you forget it."

"You don't understand," he said. "You're just like the rest of them. You don't understand a goddam thing."

She left the room. "You clean up this mess," she told him over her shoulder. "I'm not going to make the cleaning lady do it."

A little while later, Dr. Espinoza showed up and gave Harry a needle, and soon after, the anger went away.

He still couldn't stop crying, though.

It was time to go. Emily took his arm. "Honey, the limo's here." Harry Swantek, and Emily and the kids, all dressed in black clothing, some of it bought specially for this occasion, headed for the car.

• • •

Flo Ackerman's black dress had also been bought especially for the occasion. Of all the things she had expected to be doing in Harville, Pennsylvania, attending the funeral of a kidnapped and murdered government contractor was not among them.

This was a big deal. The governor was here. Both senators. The congressman, and all the state reps from the area. In this crowd, the mayor was small potatoes. The eulogy at the graveyard (the Pembrokes had an enormous family plot in the municipal cemetery—Chip would have to get busy if there were going to be enough Pembrokes around to fill it up) was the mayor's big chance, and he knew it.

Small and handsome, His Honor pulled into all the stations, with "Great American," "Great Humanitarian," "Close Personal Friend," and "Shining Example for the Youth of Today" major stops on the itinerary.

Flo checked out the crowd. Despite the density of the clichés, the speech seemed to be going over well enough. She supposed Great Men didn't die as frequently out in the boonies as they did in Washington, D.C., so maybe the citizens didn't hear the speech so often.

Flo looked for individual faces. She saw Henry Pembroke, standing ramrod stiff, with a frown that seemed engraved in his face. Chip stood by his father's side, looking younger than ever in a black suit and dark glasses.

Harry Swantek was wearing dark glasses, too, and probably for the same reason, to hide the ravages of crying. There was a delegation from the Manx Cat Society, and the National Association of Manufacturers, and Flo couldn't guess what all.

Janet stood at the back of the crowd, but as tall as she was, it was easy to spot her. Flo thought about their outing Monday night, whereat Janet had humorously and indirectly—but unmistakably—warned Flo away from her man on pain of death.

Gawky, mousy Janet had changed a lot since college. Flo guessed she had, too, and not only on the outside, but she still hadn't reached the point of actually going after married men. She managed to get that across to Janet, too.

One way she'd changed, though, was that she had no time for this. For all of this—the funerals, and the eulogies, and the sadness. What Flo wanted to know, what she was trying to decide, was how this was going to affect the career of Florence Helen Ackerman.

On the one hand, there was no doubt about it. The smoke scrubber (or whatever pretentious technical name the Agency decided to give it) was going into production. Flo had gotten Henry's signature about the matter the day after his brother's body was found. That had been her job, and the job was done, and she should be promoted, and earn numerous Brownie points with the new administration and so on and so forth and live happily ever after.

On the other hand, what a mess. Kidnapping, murder, bad publicity. And the fact that the kidnappers had solved the problem. Not her, and not her ace in the hole, the world-famous Professor Niccolo Benedetti.

Her superior had pointed that out to her in those sweet-poison terms only a woman boss could use to a woman subordinate.

Translation: Don't make waves, Florence.

On another hand, there was still Henry to be dealt with. True, he had signed the proper paper, but the man was now an emotional basket case. Since the kidnapping, he'd aged twenty years, and seemed like a man who was still alive only because he couldn't summon enough energy to die. Henry was still nominally in control of all the Pembroke corporation's numerous activities, and he could still cause trouble. Harry Swantek, who'd been for the project from the word go, was making the day-to-day decisions now, but Swantek was a mess as well, refusing consolation of any kind.

The encouragement Flo could find in that situation was the fact that Swantek (she hoped) would bounce back and get his act together relatively soon. The more she saw Henry Pembroke, the surer Flo became that *he* never would.

On the fourth hand (this thing was getting to be a regular octopus), Chip Pembroke had *already* bounced back from the trauma of finding his uncle choked to death. He was acting like the proverbial tower of strength, propping up both his father and Swantek, gently suggesting the right (from Flo's point of view) moves, and just in general holding things together. There had been a time when Flo had wondered how Chip had managed to make a success of the ice-cream company. He seemed so callow and ineffectual at first glance. She didn't wonder anymore. This situation was showing there was a lot more to Chip than met the eye. Her reports to Washington would say (appropriately hedged, of course—the first rule of government service is Cover Your Ass at All Times) that there was little to worry about if Humbert Pembroke II (no wonder he wanted everybody to call him Chip) were for any reason to assume full, active control of the family enterprises.

On the fifth and final hand (okay, not an octopus, after all), there were the developments, at least locally, in her own social life. Last night, she'd had dinner at an Italian place in Scranton with Chief Viretsky. She hadn't been so naive as to think it hadn't been at least partly business—Viretsky managed to ascertain Flo's whereabouts on several important occasions during the last few days, and he'd even dropped a couple of hints about alibis being meaningless in this kind of case because of the probability of the use of accomplices. But mostly he talked about himself, and about her, and there was definitely some interest there. The chief was not like that wife-besotted Ron Gentry, who wouldn't even engage in some harmless flirting, for God's sake.

At the end of the evening, the chief had taken her hands in his, and *almost* kissed her, and Flo thought that was kind of small-town sweet, too.

She was pretty sure she'd seen some interest in Chip's eyes, too, but of course it was too soon for him to do anything about it. It didn't matter. Flo would be around, if not continuously, the way she had been, then frequently enough. The job wasn't over by a long shot, but it shaped up as though the fringe benefits might have their points of interest.

A chorus of voices broke into Flo's thoughts. People all around her were saying "Amen," so she said "Amen," too.

• • •

"Amen," Chet Viretsky said, but he didn't bow his head. The chief hated funerals, and it was only a sense of duty that brought him out to them. Not duty as a mourner, but duty as a detective. It was one of the accepted canons of the investigative business that you can learn things at the victim's funeral if you watched the family and the mourners closely enough. So Viretsky didn't bow his head—he kept watching. Of course, all he saw when he did this were the tops of people's bowed heads, but he kept watching, anyway.

And damned if this time he *didn't* see something—Ron Gentry not bowing *his* head, scanning the crowd as assiduously as the chief himself. Their eyes met, and both men had to suppress grins. The chief told himself he had to remember to compare notes with Gentry someday. He personally had never detected a goddam thing at a funeral.

That only served to remind him that he hadn't detected a goddam thing in this whole case, except for the fact that, as so eloquently outlined the first night by Mr. Gentry, none of it made sense.

The FBI had come in after their twenty-four hours, and were being very busy and very secretive, but they hadn't learned squat, either. That was another thing Chet Viretsky had detected—he had grown good and sick of the FBI in less than two days.

The reports trickled down to him, usually twelve hours or more late, but for all the good they did, the feds might as well have held on to them. No known criminals imported into the area. No suspicious associations among anybody involved in the case. No significant scientific evidence.

In short, no nothing.

But Chet had detected a couple of other things. He detected in himself a growing case of the hots for Flo Ackerman.

The woman was tough, possibly tougher than he was, and she was making the grade in a tough racket. She was good-looking, and she wasn't shy. He'd have to watch himself until this thing got cleaned up.

Which was another reason he wished he could find a way to make Benedetti hang around.

Not that the old philosopher had been any more forthcoming than the feds. In fact, he'd been less so, since apparently philosophers don't file reports, twelve hours late or otherwise. Nevertheless, from things Ron Gentry had let slip, like the fact that the old man was grumping away in his room, fumigating himself with cigar smoke and painting or whatever the hell it was he did, Viretsky suspected he was on to something.

Any something was a whole lot more than the mess of nothing the chief found himself looking at now. He wished he could detect a way, short of bankrupting the Town of Harville, to keep Benedetti poking around into the case.

Mikta, the funeral director (and this gig undoubtedly put his firm in the black for the next couple of years), was going around passing out flowers to put on the coffin. He handed Chet a white one, pretty, of a kind he didn't recognize. The chief put it to his nose and took a sniff, but he couldn't get a smell of anything.

Typical, he thought. Just like this case.

• • •

Sandy Jovanka sniffed at the rose the guy had given her. It smelled great, but she reminded herself not to say "Mmm" or to smile at it. Sandy was getting very heady about being photographed by the press. She had been on ABC and CNN, and there was talk of her being paid actual *money* to tell the story of what went on in Omega House for one of the tabloid shows.

She wouldn't do it, though. She didn't think so, at least. She wanted to hold out for a spot on Phil Donahue. Sandy thought Phil Donahue was dreamy, for an old guy.

Anyway, even though she felt sorry for poor old Mr. Clyde Pembroke (who must have been a very great man, gosh, look at all the *photographers*), she had to admit her being in the Thick of Things had led to her being treated at long last with a little respect around this town.

It wasn't as though she were *dumb* or anything. Dumb people do not become secretaries for Pembrokes, even if it was only Chip Pembroke and his ice-cream plant they were talking about. Besides, it was very excellent ice cream. Sandy knew this to her sadness, because she was always tempted to try some, being around there and smelling it all day. Like it said on every container, "Real, rich cream, pure cane sugar, no thickeners or artificial ingredients. Ever." That made her proud, because she was a part of that quality.

Of course, real, rich cream and pure cane sugar can turn you into a blimp, and Sandy had no intention of that happening to her. Sandy came from a family of fat women cramming their feet into high heels, with fat flopping down over the sides of their shoes, and bras the size of a pair of Indian tents, and more chins than a Chinese telephone book.

Her father had said that once at Thanksgiving, that thing about the Chinese, and all the men had laughed, and the kids, too, including Sandy, but all the aunts got mad, especially Aunt Ada, who hadn't talked to Daddy for six months, until she needed somebody to pick up her new armchair at the store and Daddy was the only person she knew who had a station wagon, so she forgave him.

Anyway, Sandy had realized *real young* that it was impossible to gain weight, then go on a diet and lose it, so she decided she would go on a diet before she got fat. And it worked. She was pretty and thin all through high school, except, of course, for that horrible three months when her acne got bad, but that went away and everything was okay again.

She didn't even mind (too much) that she got a Reputation in high school. For one thing, built girls always got reputations, whether they did anything or not, and Sandy was definitely built and would not, even if somebody gave her the choice, have given up her build to avoid the reputation.

For another thing, she just happened to like boys. Boys were easier to deal with than girls. Boys might have only one thing on their minds, but Sandy at least knew *what that was.* The girls in high school, Sandy never knew what the heck *they* were thinking about. They whispered too much, and they were always laughing at jokes Sandy didn't get.

Sandy decided they were just jealous because Sandy was Built but Not Fat, and also Popular With Boys, even though she didn't put out nearly so much as everyone seemed to assume, like maybe three times altogether. She always told this to the boys she didn't have sex with, because she didn't want them to get the wrong idea that all the other guys she went out with were Getting It but not them. That would hurt their feelings.

It turned out not to matter, of course, because after Harville High, she went to secretarial school, and was near the top of her class. She was a great typist, and the teacher said she had a real gift for shorthand, not that she got to use it much, because Mr. Chips (some of the guys at the plant called Chip Pembroke that behind his back, but Sandy never did because it wasn't respectful) hardly ever dictated anything to her live—he always had some kind of recording dictaphone gadget, new ones all the time, that she had to use.

That was a nuisance (so was working Saturdays), but she put up with it because the rest of the job was so good.

Also, she liked Chip Pembroke. He could have done like a lot of rich boys and lived like a playboy in Scranton or even

New York on his allowance, but instead he hung around town and made jobs for people. Family tradition, sort of.

He was even cute in a nerdy sort of way. Sandy could tell he liked her, too, or at least he liked looking at her, and he treated her very nice, like a gentleman.

Maybe too much like a gentleman. After all, his mother hadn't even been a secretary, according to the story, just a factory worker, for crying out loud. Oh, God, wouldn't it be something to wind up Mrs. Pembroke? Of course, *Chip* had to do something about that first. He was so shy. Either that, or he was scared by sexual harassment stuff.

Sandy was all for women's rights, because she was a woman, wasn't she? But she sometimes wondered what the feminist leaders were going on about. I mean, the only way for a secretary like herself to make it Really Big was to marry the boss, and how could that happen if he was even afraid to ask you out?

The idea was to help women, right? So how does it help women to scare guys with money away from them, that's what Sandy wanted to know. For crying out loud, she was not going to make it to the top in the ice-cream business. She didn't even *eat* ice cream, because if she did, she would be genetically doomed to FAT. Didn't these big-time feminists ever think of *that*?

Anyway, there was another way to make it big, and that was to get famous. A good way to do that was to sleep with somebody famous like an evangelist or a future president or something and then tell about it. But like in high school, Sandy was just not That Kind of Girl. Much. But maybe being a witness in a murder case could do it. Maybe she could get a book out of this, or a modeling thing, or learn how to sing. Or even act.

She knew you had to prepare for that, but she already was. She'd spent hours finding a black dress that was modest but would still show she was Built. And, now, for practice, maybe she could manage a tear as she put her flower on the coffin.

She thought of her ankles spilling over her shoes, and it worked. Sandy just hoped the cameras were rolling.

T h r e e

The sun came out just about the time the last blossom hit the coffin. It occurred to Ron that this was the first time he'd seen it since he'd come to Harville five days before.

The crowd noticed it, too, and it added to the air of relief, if not happiness, that comes with the end of a funeral. Ron took Janet's arm and headed for the car. The Professor followed along, quietly.

Then a voice behind them. "Professor?"

They turned to see Chip Pembroke.

"Mr. Pembroke," Benedetti said softly. "My condolences. And my apologies."

"Apologies?" Chip looked confused.

"My presence did nothing to save you and your father from these sad events."

Chip shrugged it off. "You couldn't have foreseen—"

Benedetti gave him a sad shrug. "I have become accustomed to a high standard for myself. I must be the judge of whether I have met it."

"Of course. But if you could wait a moment, my father would like to talk to you."

"I owe him that much."

Chip led the way. Ron and Janet weren't specifically invited, but they went anyway. Henry Pembroke was still standing at the grave site, his back to the catafalque.

"Thank you, Professor," he said when they approached.

"I have done nothing."

"Your advice got me through . . . this." Henry Pembroke looked especially pale today. The purple mark on his wrist had been joined by several on his face, and they stood out against his white skin like jelly on a tablecloth.

"The sun feels good," Pembroke continued. "It's not appropriate, but it feels good."

"Advice is always cheap to the giver of it. I am glad it has helped you."

"Yes. The question, Professor, is what am I going to do now?"

"Surely that is a question you must answer for yourself."

"For myself, I have answered it. I am still following your advice. You told me to hold on to my anger. Right now, that anger is all I have. I am determined to find whoever has done this and make them pay."

"That is your privilege, sir."

"I want you to help me do it."

"Niccolo Benedetti does not *help* find *malfattori*, eh? I study evil and the perpetrators of it. And only when I have been asked."

"I am asking you."

"Are you sure? You must be very sure. Once started, I will not be swayed, whatever the results."

"I *want* results."

"You may not like them."

"I want the people who killed my brother. My twin brother. There is no closer relationship, Professor. When we fought with each other, it was because we were unhappy with ourselves. We—I—have done some foolish things in my life, and I'll pay for them. But the thought of my brother being deliberately strangled—I start to choke, myself. I'm saying this badly."

"Not at all."

"All I can say is that it's as if I've been murdered myself. The difference is, I'm still around to do something about it. I have no talent in that direction, no genius. All I have is money and influence. They will be put at your disposal to the limit. Do this for me. Please."

Ron, by this time, was puzzled. Since the murder, Benedetti had shown no interest in *life*, much less the case. Ron had assumed that despite the facets of the case that didn't make sense, the Professor had decided the whole business had been the work of a bunch of ham-fisted incompetents with an urge for easy money and delusions of grandeur, a common kind of criminal, and a kind in which the old man had absolutely no interest.

So Ron had been surprised at the Professor's stringing Henry along like that. Benedetti could play cat and mouse with the best of them, but he was seldom cruel.

Then the old man said, "Very well," and Ron wanted to hug him. Henry Pembroke, too. The millionaire's face broke into a weak but genuine smile, as if his smile muscles had been called out of retirement, and were game but out of practice.

"However," the Professor said, "I must ask your son's opinion, as well."

Henry Pembroke looked startled. "Why, Chip wants what I want. Don't you, Chip?"

Benedetti asked, "Do you?"

"What? Sure. Of course. Like Dad says, I want this guy caught. After all, they might have killed me, too. Sometimes I'm surprised they didn't." Chip shook his head.

"You must thank God for your deliverance. And I must thank you for your commission. I cannot, however, engage to do this any longer from a suite in the Harville Inn."

It took a little hinting around, but, in the end, the Professor maneuvered the surviving Pembrokes, as he had Clyde before them, into inviting him and Ron and Janet (and, he supposed, Nimrod) to use Alpha House and the servants thereof for as long as he needed them.

The Professor thanked them and bowed, and they headed for the car.

• • •

"Professor," Ron said, as he made his way from the cemetery an hour later, "I hate to admit this, but I'm not up to you."

"There is no reason you should be, *amico*. I have taught you to fathom many things, but you will always find it difficult to fathom me. I can hardly do it myself."

Benedetti leaned back in his seat. "Ronald, Janet, I have a confession to make."

"*Maestro*, are you feeling all right?"

"I am feeling," he said, "better than I have in days. That is the point. My behavior since the morning after Clyde Pembroke's body was found has not been the moody workings of my genius. It has been the petulant sulking of a child."

"You weren't so bad," Janet said. "You just weren't around much."

Benedetti smiled the kind of warm smile he seemed to save only for Janet. "Believe me, *cara amica*, in the privacy of my own room, I was very bad indeed. I was bad to the point of becoming disgusted with myself."

"What was the problem?"

"I was wallowing in the sin of Pride. I had a desperate desire for something for which my conceit would not let me ask."

"To stay on the case," Janet said.

"Precisely. My reputation, and therefore my effectiveness, have come to depend on a perceived aloofness on my part to any one particular crime. This ensures cooperation. It ensures that our efforts, being the harder to come by, will be more appreciated."

He reached for his pocket and took out a cigar. Then he looked at it, frowned, and put it back. To Janet, he said,

"Forgive me. I shall refrain from smoking in this enclosed space."

Ron was getting nervous. This was not the Benedetti he knew. Before this, the Professor didn't give a damn whom he grossed out with his cigars. Next thing you knew, he'd even be reaching for a dinner check. It wasn't that Ron wouldn't like to see the old man a little more considerate; it was that he was worried that a change in personality would be the first step in the dissolution of one of the century's most amazing minds.

"*Va bene*," the old man went on. "So I would not bring myself to ask to continue, though Chief Viretsky dropped less-than-subtle hints that he would appreciate our staying. And, yet, what compelled me to *want* to continue was also pride."

"I wasn't too crazy about having a kidnapping and murder pulled off under my nose, either."

"It wasn't just that, Ronald. There was something about the events that occurred that night, something not right. You reflected the unease yourself."

"I haven't felt right since I got here."

Benedetti slapped his thigh. "Well," he said. "Chief Viretsky wanted us, the Pembrokes wanted us. Now, they have got us."

"So what do we do, *Maestro*?" Ron asked.

"Today, we paint, plan, and pack. Tomorrow morning, we will relocate to Alpha House. I have a few requests to make of the chief. Ron, you talk to everyone again. Janet, you will spend the day researching the Pembrokes, with emphasis on the brothers. Could they have aroused the type of hatred that would cause someone to ignore a million dollars in cash?"

Janet knitted her brows for a second, then said, "Oh. *Oh.* You mean, the express purpose of the whole operation may have been to murder Clyde?"

The Professor nodded. "And to cause suffering to Henry as well. And Chip. Do not forget the last of the Pembrokes."

"I'd like to meet the person," Ron said, "no matter how rich, who could walk away from a million dollars in cash."

"We may," the Professor said impassively, "already have met the person."

• • •

Back at the inn, the Professor hightailed it back to his room.

"Ready to start painting," Janet suggested after he was gone.

"Either that, or he was dying for a cigar." Ron turned on the TV to a Big East college football game, and began to pack.

"Be sure to leave out things we need for tomorrow," Janet said.

"Right. Um, aren't you going to help?"

"In a little while. I have to sit for a few minutes. Do you mind?"

Ron said of course not, and Janet plopped down into an armchair and watched the screen as though she had a lot of money bet on Rutgers against West Virginia with the points. She kicked off her shoes.

Ron made conversation as he stuffed things in suitcases. "He's never passed up a cigar before. I think you're probably his favorite person."

"He puts up with me because you love me."

"No, that's why *I* put up with you." Ron walked around the chair and kissed her on the lips.

Janet said, "Mmm. Maybe. But the Professor *is* more perceptive than you are."

"Of course he is. That's why he's the Professor."

"He notices more about your life than you do."

"If you are talking about Flo Ackerman, I plead innocent."

Janet arched an eyebrow. "Innocent? Of what?"

"Of anything! I'm innocent in the childlike sense. That's an admirable trait."

"Yes, dear." Janet fought a smile and lost.

"Besides," Ron went on, "am I not a better person for not suspecting every woman I meet of wanting my body, for God's sake?"

"Well, you're certainly a better person than if you thought every woman you met *did*," Janet conceded.

"Okay, then. So enough about what a jerk I am not to have seen Flo coming on to me. And, besides, I still don't think she did."

"She did," Janet said. "She's admitted as much to me. But that's—"

"Wait a minute. You went to dinner last night, and Flo told you she took a run at your husband?"

"She didn't think of it as a run. Just sort of a few jogging steps. Girls who grow up thinking of themselves as homely have a tough time believing great-looking guys are anything but slime."

"There are so many things wrong with that, I don't know where to start."

"Let it go, then, because what I really want to talk to you about—"

"I think the Professor should let Evil slide for a while, and try to figure out women."

"Well," Janet said slyly, "the Professor's figured out enough not to light his cigar."

Ron sat on the edge of the bed. "I give up."

"It's simple, dear. This is confession day. Benedetti made his confession; here's mine: I'm pregnant."

"Pregnant. Like you and me are going to have a baby together?"

"Yup."

"No fooling?"

"Nope."

There were some words said in the next five minutes, and though none of them was especially coherent, they were all joyous. Ron scooped Janet out of the chair, spun her around a couple of times and plunked her down on the bed, very, very gently. There were kisses and hugs and squeals of delight.

". . . and if it's a boy, we'll call it Niccolo, and if it's a girl, Niccolette, and—"

"I'll kill you." Janet laughed and bopped him on the head.

"I was only kidding. Honest. I don't even think the Professor can stretch his pride far enough to rejoice in a kid named 'Niccolo Gentry.'"

"Okay, then."

"How far along are you? When did you know?"

"About two months. I found out shortly after you took off for Canada."

"We talked on the phone every night. Why didn't you tell me?"

"Because I wanted to tell you in person. After I got here, there hardly seemed a good time to do it. I wanted everything to be perfect."

"Darling," Ron said, "if you waited for everything to be perfect, the kid would be on his way to college before I ever knew he was coming. Or on her way."

"You're the detective. You would have figured it out eventually."

"I suppose so. As you say, I have been a little slow on the uptake lately. So that's why the Professor spurned his cigar. I wonder how he knew."

"Don't ask him."

"I won't ask him. But we've got to tell him. Officially, I mean. In a little while. Certainly, before we tell anyone else."

"Of course."

"How are you? Have you been throwing up mornings when I haven't noticed?"

"No, nothing like that, thank God. Yet. I just get a little snappy. Maybe you've noticed."

"Maybe a little. I thought you were mad at me about something I hadn't figured out yet."

"Nope."

"God, this is great."

"You're really happy?"

"Happy? I'm ecstatic. How about you?"

"Same here. Now you know why I didn't come down here right away."

"I do?"

"Cats. I knew I was pregnant, and I knew we'd inevitably be exposed to cats, so, of course, I couldn't come until I'd had my test for toxoplasmosis."

"Oh, right. That's the disease you get from cat doo."

Janet smiled at him. "How scientific."

"From feline feces. Happy now? It seems like a cold or the flu, but it can cause brain damage in unborn— Hey, what the hell are we doing with Nimrod in here? He's been all over us for a couple of days!"

"Relax, honey. That was the point of the test. Toxoplasmosis is one of those things you can only get once. I was sure I'd had it at one point or the other as a kid—we always had a cat around the house—but, of course, I had to be sure. So I had a blood test, and it turned out I've got the antibodies, so we don't have anything to worry about on that score."

"Why take chances?" Ron asked. "We can get you a kitten after the baby is born."

"Don't you like Nimrod?"

"I like him better than anything else that's ever ruined my shoes, but that's not the point. The point is our child. You're going to be a terrific mother."

"That's right, I am. And you ought to know that I wouldn't take the slightest chance of hurting our child."

"Of course not, but—"

"But nothing. The doctor said I could take up lion-taming if I wanted, so far as my immunity to feline feces was concerned."

"All right, then." Ron kissed her again. "Let's get this wrapped up so we can get back home and start planning a nursery."

"Deal," Janet said. "I've got an idea I want to check out, anyway."

"What is it?"

"I'll tell you tomorrow. You and the Professor aren't the only ones who get to be mysterious around here."

F o u r

The one and only time the late Sophie Havelka Pembroke had seen the small three-room suite up under the eaves of Omega House that was occupied by Lewis Jackson, she had been horrified. She had given the decorator (number four, as Jackson remembered it) specific instructions about making *all* the rooms conform to the futuristic scheme of the place.

That had been done, and it had lasted about half a day. Jackson had personally carried the chrome and pastel stuff to the attic, painted over the lime-green walls with no-nonsense white, and filled the room with solid, comfortable furniture made of God's own wood.

When Mrs. Pembroke poked in to check up on the decorator, and saw a normal man doing normal work in a normal room, she screamed that he was fired. How dare he do this to her?

Jackson showed her the calm face he showed everyone, no matter what turmoil he was going through. For a black man of Jackson's generation, it was one way to survive while keeping one's self-respect intact.

"I'm sorry, ma'am," he said, not sounding sorry at all, "but I couldn't work or sleep in this place the way you had it. I need a comfortable home, or I won't be worth my salary."

"You're not worth anything!" She had a pretty face, but it was ugly when she was being mean. That was why she was very careful to keep her meanness away from the view of Mr. Henry Pembroke. "And you don't work here anymore, either, do you understand? Pack your things."

Jackson remained impassive. "Yes, ma'am. But I work for

Mr. Pembroke, for both Mr. Pembrokes, you see, and have been since before you came along. As soon as I hear from one of them, I'll start packing. But until I *am* fired, I still have work to do, so good afternoon."

He closed the door on her. It was a good, solid, thick door (somehow, none of the decorators had gotten around to purging it), but he could still hear her cursing as she went down the stairs.

He sighed, and figured he might as well start packing, at that. Mrs. Pembroke had a way of being sweet when she wanted to be, and she plain sweeted her husband into doing the most foolish things you could think of. This house, for instance. Jackson sighed again, and went back to his adding machine to figure the maintenance accounts.

Now, here it was, forty-odd years later, and he was still doing maintenance accounts on that same adding machine. There had been offers over the years to provide him with everything from a pocket calculator to a personal computer, but Jackson had turned them all down. Punch, punch, punch, pull the lever. The rhythm soothed him somehow, and he'd never had any complaints about the accuracy of his figures. That was the trouble with people. They wanted something different before they appreciated what they had.

Lewis Jackson appreciated the good things he had. Like good people to work for. They paid him well, and treated him with respect. So much respect, in fact, that Jackson had never heard another word about being fired, not from the Pembroke brothers or from anybody else. In that one thing, at least, Mr. Henry Pembroke hadn't let his wife sweet him into doing wrong, or shrew him into it, either. Jackson had appreciated that. That kind of loyalty and respect was important to him.

Of course, they weren't his *friends*. The life Jackson had

led didn't lead to friendship, as such. He didn't mind. He'd provided top-notch service to the Pembrokes—keeping their houses staffed, supervising the planting and the mowing of the landscaped portions of the estate, doing whatever needed to be done when it needed to be done, even more or less raising Chip.

In fact, in Jackson's mind, he *had* raised Chip. The boy's mother hadn't been interested, and now she was gone. Chip's father, with all due respect, hadn't been cut out to look after a child, either. Chip's Uncle Clyde and Jackson himself had been the major influences over the boy. Together, they tried to make him feel less lonely and scared, which, wealth or no wealth, Chip certainly had been.

Now, Mr. Clyde Pembroke was dead, Mr. Henry Pembroke was—well, Jackson didn't like to think about what Mr. Henry was, these days—and that left him to watch out for a boy (Jackson still thought of Chip as a boy) who was soon going to be very alone and very rich.

They'd do fine together. Because behind his impassive face, Lewis Jackson loved Chip as much as any father loved any son.

Nobody knew Lewis Jackson well enough to be able to discern that, and Jackson wasn't the type to tell. It was possible even Chip didn't know it. Well, someday he would.

Jackson looked at the clock, carefully tore the figures off the adding machine roll, flattened them, and put them in their file in the filing cabinet he'd used for the estate's accounts since he'd started doing them.

He took a set of car keys from a row of hooks by the door. He had another little errand to do for the Pembrokes.

F i v e

Mr. Jackson came in the black Town Car to pick up all their stuff, certainly the most elegant moving van with which Ron had ever been associated. Janet and the Professor rode with Jackson, while Ron took Nimrod in the rented car. When they reached the gravel drive up through the woods, the cat swished his tail stump angrily, and made loud protests at the jouncing.

"Come on," Ron said. "You've been over this at least twice before."

The kitten meowed again; Ron said, "Boy, if you could talk, this case would be over."

Nimrod seemed pleased at that idea. In any case, he settled down in the bottom of the cat carrier Ron had dashed out to buy that morning and went to sleep.

After they got settled in their rooms at Alpha House, Janet was off for her work in the newspaper morgue, and on her own private project, whatever the hell that was. She'd turn in the rental car at their office near the newspaper. Ron would pick her up later, and they'd do some shopping.

As she drove off, Ron turned from the window and said to the Professor, "My God, I'm becoming something I never could tolerate."

"What is that, *amico*?"

"One of those expectant fathers, like in the movies. Janet's driving off alone, and I'm scared to death over what might happen to her."

"Janet will be fine."

"I know that. It's just that all of a sudden, I don't believe it."

"It was a very smooth ride coming up here today, comparatively speaking," the old man said.

"Depends on the car. I was bouncing so badly, Nimrod couldn't even meow straight. You were in a land yacht. The suspension in that one costs more than the car I was driving. That kind of thing makes all the difference."

"Yes, I suppose it does. Are my paints convenient?"

"On top of the dresser near the big window. I put your easel up there. I know you like the light."

"When I can get it."

Ron was looking out the window. Janet was out of sight now. Ron worried some more.

"My God," he said. "She hasn't been gone two minutes. How am I going to last seven more months?"

"I have noticed a tendency in you to worry too much, my friend. You must try to calm down."

"*Maestro*, we are talking about a woman who spends a good portion of her working life locked in a small room with a succession of crazy people."

"None of whom has ever hurt her in the slightest."

"That I know of. What the hell, she waited a week and a half to tell me she was pregnant. She's got some angle on the case she won't tell me about. What else is she keeping from me? For all I know, she's had to shoot seventeen violent patients. She's very staunch on confidentiality, you know. Miss Ethics I had to marry."

"Miss Ethics you *wanted* to marry."

Ron grinned. "I sure did. I've never regretted it for a second. But I'm afraid this fatherhood thing might be a little too big for me."

"Nonsense. Niccolo Benedetti would not pick a student who was not equal to any task that might befall a man, let alone the most basic of all. As a father, as at everything else, you will be all a person could want."

"Wow," Ron said. "I'm touched. Thank you, *Maestro*."

"It is a mark of the corruption of our society and our language," the Professor said, "that one man should feel moved to thank another for telling the truth. We will say no more about it. Come with me. I will smoke in my room."

The Professor got his cigar lit the instant he was over the threshold. He went and put a canvas on the blackboard. It was early stages yet, but what there was, was a kind of circle with lines in it, a blotchy orange-red takeoff on the peace symbol of the sixties.

"I will work on this today," he announced. "You will occupy yourself with work likewise; it will help you keep your mind off your worries."

"As you say, *Maestro*. See you later."

As he left, however, Ron already had something to keep his mind off his worries. He couldn't make head or tail of what the Professor's canvas was supposed to represent—neither could the old man, yet, probably. But that wasn't the important part. The important part was that on each case, Benedetti's work began representational, and, as the case progressed, got more and more abstract. What Ron had seen looked very abstract indeed. That meant the old man was a lot further along than he was.

He's supposed to be teaching me his technique, Ron thought, but I still have a long way to go.

• • •

It was the second consecutive day of sunshine, there was a nice fall crispness to the air, and Ron decided to stroll over to Omega House, which was his first port of call for the afternoon.

It was much easier going than it had been that first evening. Less spooky, too. There was nothing in the air but the smoky smell of fall (Chip must be using some tamer flavor than grape at the factory today), and he had birdcalls, melodic or comically raucous, to keep him company all the way through the woods.

Ron stopped, with Omega House in sight.

Birdcalls.

All the way through the woods.

Ron ran back into the former dead zone and listened. And looked. No doubt about it, birds were back. He saw plenty of them, and heard even more. He ran on to Omega House.

When Jackson opened the door, Ron asked to use a phone. He immediately called the Professor and told him what he'd discovered.

"Excellent, *amico*. As I said, all anyone could desire. It was a wise thing to check the woods, but I did not think to tell you to do so. So you did."

"I didn't think of it. I just did it."

"Even better. You have so internalized my needs that fulfilling them has become a species of instinct with you."

"Very funny. The point is, what does it mean?"

"I do not know. I do not think the reappearance can be of any less significance than their disappearance was."

"But we don't know what that was all about, either, do we?"

"No, we don't. On that point, I am absolutely baffled."

"Just on that one point?" Ron wanted to know. "On the other points, you're not baffled?"

"Thank you for calling, Ronald."

"Professor—"

"Good-bye."

The connection broke. Ron looked at the receiver for a few seconds, as though it might tell him something on its own, then hung up. The old man was turning coy. Maddeningly coy.

This is good, Ron thought. This is more like the old, pain-in-the-ass him.

He went to look up Mr. Jackson.

• • •

Ron roamed Omega House. The sci-fi atmosphere of the place was so strong, he felt as if he ought to be wearing a space suit. He finally followed a whirring noise to a basement workshop, where he found Jackson holding what looked at first to Ron like a free-form chrome sculpture, but that he soon recognized as the frame for one of those godforsaken ultramodern lamp tables that dotted the house above. With grim determination (he was probably sick of the things, too, Ron reflected), Jackson bent over the object with safety-goggled eyes and buffed away at it with an electric buffing wheel, whose motor made the whirring Ron had heard.

"Mr. Jackson?" Ron said. "I'd like to ask you a few questions."

"Why me?" Jackson demanded. He pushed his goggles to the top of his head.

"We've been ignoring you," Ron said. "Or you've been eluding us. The FBI and the cops had only the most superficial discussion with you, and you've managed to elude the press completely."

"Maybe I like it that way."

"Maybe so. But you're a resource I can't afford to waste. You're right here, you've *been* right here through all of it, before the Professor and me, before Miss Ackerman, even. You're a smart man, and you're obviously much more than a servant."

"You hesitated before you said the word 'servant,'" Jackson pointed out. "Do I make you uncomfortable, Mr. Gentry? The old black family retainer and all that?"

"Well, to be frank, yeah. Though I think enough of myself to believe that 'black' is the smallest part of that."

Jackson chuckled. "I believe you, Mr. Gentry. Rest assured, I like what I'm doing. For one thing, I don't see myself as serving Mr. Henry Pembroke. I manage a vast estate. I arrange for the landscaping, the maintenance, the vehicles. I hire the rest of the staff—if I did this for a country club or something, I'd be in the newspapers as a pioneer. Because I do it for a private individual, I'm some kind of embarrassment. All I really am is a man doing a job. That's all I've ever been."

"I don't even know your first name."

"Lewis. Lewis James Jackson. Born Easter Sunday, 1926. Went to work for the Pembroke brothers in 1946, after I got out of the army. I was the loading dock foreman from 1955 to 1963, and there was some mess about that when it started. Some of the men didn't want to take orders from a Negro (we were Negroes then, if you were being polite), but Mr. Pembroke, both of them, stuck by me, and I won the boys over, even if I had to whup them, which I did once or twice."

"What happened in 1963?"

"Got knocked off the dock by a crane, you know. Landed funny and broke my back. Pembrokes paid for everything. Fortunately, I got the use of all my limbs back. But I couldn't lift anything. You're no use around a loading dock if you can't lift anything. They gave me a good pension, which I still get, then Mr. Henry Pembroke said if I wanted to, I could come and be foreman of the family estate. That's how he put it, and that's how I think of it. And I've been doing it ever since."

"Good bosses."

"Good men."

"What was Mrs. Pembroke like?"

Jackson's face set like a mask, and his voice went cold.

"I don't choose to talk about Mrs. Pembroke."

"That bad, huh?"

"It's not my place to talk about Mrs. Pembroke."

"Your *place*? You sure slipped the servant's livery on quick there, when you wanted to."

The mask slipped off, and Jackson smiled patiently at him. "You're not going to bait me, Mr. Gentry. I won't talk about the woman. Anything you ask, you should ask Mr. Pembroke."

"How about Chip?"

"I can't stop you. And I don't mean to tell you your business, but don't you think it'd be a little silly asking a man about his own mother?"

"Nonono, I've given up on her. I meant, 'How about Chip?' Is he a good man like his uncles? He's the heir apparent, isn't he? How's the town going to fare with Chip in the patriarch's seat? How are *you* going to do?"

"I will do fine under any circumstances. I am old enough to retire, and I have enough money put by to last me as long as God lets me live."

"Come on, Mr. Jackson. I'm not trying to get a story for the *Enquirer*, I'm trying to find a way to the truth of a vicious crime."

Jackson looked suspicious. "What kind of way? All these questions seem sort of sneaky, like you're looking for dirt."

"Well, I'll admit they're sneaky. It happens to private detectives; we get suspicious and we get sneaky. Here's what I'm driving at. As far as I can tell, the Pembroke brothers are paragons of capitalism. I haven't been able to find anyone outside the family who'll say a word against them. I mean, Harville doesn't even have a town radical in it."

Jackson chuckled. "Oh, there were a few. Weekly paper they sold to the young folks, just trying to stir up trouble. Outsiders published it. Called it *Starchild* or some such nonsense. Said the Pembrokes were paternalistic plutocrats, or something like that, ran the town like feudal lords. Called me an Uncle Tom and their house nigger. Didn't ask me a thing about it, first, though. You know something? I've been black a long time now, and when I was growing up in Tennessee, I heard lots of names. But since I left the army and came to work in Harville, that underground rag was the only thing or person that called me a nigger and got away with it."

Jackson sat back in his seat. "So, as I say, there used to be. They sort of drifted away when the recession came on hard, and a lot of companies moved their factories overseas. Paternalistic plutocrats look pretty good to a man who's working when his friend in the next town's about spent his last unemployment check."

"Okay," Ron conceded. "The Pembroke brothers are popular, even loved. So maybe nobody did this thing to hurt them. Maybe it was done to hurt Chip."

"What do you mean?" Jackson's eyes were suddenly narrow and wary.

"I mean, does Chip Pembroke have any enemies? Was he wild as a kid, maybe with girls? You raised him, as far as I can tell. Could he have made somebody, possibly a crazy somebody, hate him enough to hurt his family this way?"

"Seems like it would be more to the point to kill Chip, then. Or his daddy." He shook his head. "God forgive me for talking this way."

"There's a big difference between talking about something and doing it, Mr. Jackson. As for Clyde being the one who was kidnapped, maybe the kidnapper couldn't tell which was which. It's probably difficult to see that birthmark in the dark."

Ron didn't add that the kidnapper got Clyde outside the cattery, a place at which bird lover Henry wouldn't be caught dead. Oops. Poor choice of words. Ron winced internally, and went on.

"So you see what I'm driving at. Can you help me?"

"I don't know." It occurred to Ron that if Jackson didn't have such enormous natural self-possession, he'd be jumping around and cursing just now. The old man hated something about this conversation, just *hated* it, and wanted Ron to stop.

But a good private eye *can't* stop. "You'd know if anybody would," Ron said.

"That's just it. I don't think anybody *would*. Since he's grown up, Chip's spent most of his time . . . oh, treading water. I know he's forty years old, but it's like he's still not grown up yet. He's never really been *encouraged* to grow up, except by—" Jackson bit his lip, then went on. "Oh, he's shown signs of it, with his ice-cream business and all. That's a good product, by the way."

"I've heard," Ron said. "Except by whom?"

"Pardon me?"

"Who was it who encouraged Chip to grow up? Was it you?"

Jackson was defiant. "As a matter of fact, it was. What of it?"

"Nothing. I'm all for growing up. Like the ice-cream business?"

"Yes. Well, until he started that, he never did much of anything, just fooled around. You asked me about him as a kid. I assume you mean as a teenager, and those times."

"That's right."

"Well, he wasn't wild. Used to make me worry, sometimes. A teenage boy wants to get into devilment; it's not natural for him to hold it all in. I guess he figured his mother was—"

Jackson's lips snapped shut with an audible click.

Ron prompted, "Using up the family's devilment allotment all by herself."

Jackson shook his head. "I won't talk about that woman. You talk to Mr. Henry Pembroke. He's the one to tell you, if he chooses to."

"I'll do that. Anyway, it looks like Chip will have his swings in the big leagues soon enough."

"What do you mean?"

"For all the exercise, his father doesn't seem very well, especially over the last couple of days."

"The man's twin brother has been *murdered*."

"I know," Ron said. "And I don't deny it's a factor. But it's more than that."

Jackson let out a breath, but said nothing.

"Isn't it?"

Jackson stared at Ron for a good fifteen seconds, a hard, angry stare.

Ron had gotten a lot of them over the years, but this one gave him an itch in the small of his back. He thought of several things to say to defend himself, but he let them pass, choosing instead to meet the stare.

At last, Jackson said, "That's something else you better ask Mr. Pembroke."

"Yeah. Thank you for your time, Mr. Jackson."

"Mr. Gentry, I wouldn't have your job for all the money in the world." Jackson pulled the glasses down over his eyes, and applied the buffer so hard Ron could smell the fabric of the spinning head begin to burn.

Ron said good-bye and walked away, but Jackson ignored him.

As he climbed the narrow basement stairs, Ron sucked his lower lip and thought. Somebody with a low-down, dirty, suspicious mind could construct a motive out of the conversation he'd just had with Jackson.

Suppose the old man, raised poor, now surrounded by enormous wealth he can see and touch but never own, *identifies* with Chip Pembroke, the heir to all this money, power, and (at least on a local level) near-feudal majesty. Suppose further, he's decided that Chip has come of age to run the show. Wouldn't it make sense, then, to clear out the Pembroke brothers? Not only would that bring Chip into his glory, it would leave Jackson as Chip's *only trusted adviser.* Jackson could be the power behind the throne, and laugh at everybody. *And* he'd have a secret million dollars—or a share of it—squirreled away for a rainy day.

Near the top of the stairs, Ron asked himself if he really believed it.

No, he didn't believe it. But he knew he couldn't forget it, either. Ron decided he'd have to make sure Viretsky wasn't neglecting to find out if there was anybody around Jackson knew who'd go for kidnapping and/or murder for a million bucks or a share thereof. Just in case.

Ron was shaking his head as he left the basement and returned to the sunlight flooding the windows of Omega House.

Sometimes he didn't care much for his job, either.

S i x

Surprise, surprise, Janet thought, the Pembrokes do *not* own the local paper. Still, they swung enough weight in the town that their name was the magic word that gave her the freedom of the morgue, and for the last hour and a half, the assistance of a local intern named Diane. Diane, a junior at Harville High School, was assistant editor of the school paper, and she saw journalism as something not far short of a Divine Calling.

"It's so thrilling," she'd said, "to make sure people know the *truth*." The teenager was so serious and so enthralled with the idea of it all (and so much like Janet herself at the same age, being tall, bespectacled, and gawky), that Janet couldn't help liking her. She just hoped Diane's career actually did get some Truth across and not, like most of the media these days, just the opinion that happened to be the Flavor of the Month.

Anyway, Janet looked at miles of microfilm and acres of newsprint that hadn't been microfilmed yet.

"I understand next year everything is going on laser disk," Diane told her.

"I'd better be done with this by next year," Janet said.

At times, though, it didn't seem as if she would be. The Pembrokes got mentioned in the Harville paper more often than the president got mentioned in the *New York Times*. She saw everything—PEMBROKES DEDICATE MUNICIPAL POOL; PEMBROKES KICK OFF MARCH OF DIMES; PEMBROKES BUY INDIANA WASHER FACTORY; MRS. HENRY PEMBROKE DIES IN CAR CRASH. That from about eleven years ago. Janet pursued it, but Sophie's death was plain reckless driving, as far as anyone could tell at the time.

Looking at the photos of Sophie's crumpled car, Janet reflected on the strange turn her own life had taken. She had found love because of murder. Her marriage had grown and strengthened because she and her husband shared the investigation of murder. They were celebrating the news of their impending child in the middle of murder.

A year from now, would she be nursing a child while looking through documents, trying to get into the mind of a killer? What kind of childhood were they planning here?

She shook her head. The thing to remember was that she—and Ron and, of course, the Professor—were the good guys. Her child would learn the difference between good guys and bad. And if the kid might be exposed to the knowledge of some terrible things at a young age, he or she would also know there were things you could do. You didn't have to just shrug and walk away and be glad it happened to somebody else. You could do something about evil.

She stuck with it, and she got to the end of the clips. She had a lot of details, but no new insights on the Pembroke family, except that in all the publicity over the years, Chip was virtually absent. Possibly through his own choice. It has to be tough being the child of anybody famous.

But then you didn't need a Ph.D. in psychology to tell you that.

You also didn't need any advanced degrees to know that if the Pembroke brothers had been in the movie business instead of heavy industry, the tabloids would have had a party with the late Mrs. Henry, despite the *Harville Record*'s consistent tiptoeing around potential scandal.

Janet wondered if she ought to urge Diane to read this stuff, just to see how much journalism has changed.

Anyway, she really hadn't learned anything new. That was

a shame, but not a catastrophe. As she had hinted to Ron, she had something else in mind. Something that might actually have a bearing on the case. Something that *she* had thought of first.

Janet had, in recent years, formed the ambition to beat—just once—the Professor and Ron to the solution of a case. Just to prove something, probably to herself. This wouldn't do that, of course, but it would be a step in the right direction. A *conscious* contribution to a case, instead of the unconscious ones she usually made.

She asked Diane if there was a phone she could use in private. The girl showed her to a small office in the back of the morgue. Janet took her phone credit card out of her purse. Then she began to run up expenditures worthy of the Professor himself.

• • •

Ron picked her up just about the time she was done.

"How was the canary?"

"Oh, do I look smug?" she asked disingenuously.

"That's how you look, all right. This have to do with your private hunch, by any chance?"

"As a matter of fact, it does."

"Must have worked out."

"Mmm-hmm."

"Great feeling, isn't it?"

"Yes!" Then she thought about it. "I mean, no. I mean it's great to have my hunch confirmed, but it's not so nice to find out what I found out."

Ron showed her a crooked grin while he polished his glasses. "Get used to it, sweetheart. If you're going to go around having hunches, you've got to concentrate on the first and forget the second."

"Sounds hard."

"Takes practice," Ron conceded. "When do the Professor and I get to hear it?"

"Right away," Janet said. "You do, at least. In the car. This is nothing to blab in a newspaper office."

She pulled the door open, to see Diane scooting away as though she had something very important to do. Her neck was very, very red. Janet figured the kid would go far in the news business.

Ron slammed his door, got his seat belt on, then looked at Janet. "Okay," he said. "Buckle up, then let me have it."

"All right," she said. "I had to use every connection I had, and every trick I could think of to get this, but I did. I'm almost one hundred percent sure that Henry Pembroke has AIDS."

"He does," Ron said.

"You see, I saw the purple splotches, the main one on his wrist, but others. I figured at first that was a birthmark, like his brother's, but I had forgotten that the mark on Clyde's forehead—I only saw it once, remember. . . ."

Janet shuddered at the memory of the strangled Clyde, the purple mark almost lost in the purplish tinge of the face, and the overhead glare of the lamp.

"I had forgotten that the mark on Clyde's forehead was a *forceps* mark, not a natural birthmark at all. Then I realized there was no reason for Henry to have the purple marks on his skin unless there's something wrong with him. Then, when we saw him at the cemetery, so weak and sickly, something clicked. I thought *purple blotches*—Kaposi's sarcoma—AIDS.

"Now, I figured that if Henry were being treated for this at all, it wouldn't be here, it would be in New York, so I called a friend of mine who's a big society doctor there, and I asked him who a prominent man who wanted secrecy would go to and he gave me a list and—"

Janet closed her mouth and ran the tape back in her mind. She glanced at her husband. "What did you say?" she demanded.

"Nothing. Go on, this is great work."

"You said, 'He does.'"

"I did?"

"Don't tease me, dammit." She wanted to hit him. "How long have you known?"

"Found out today. Just before I came here. Probably just about the same time you did."

"Damn, damn, damn. How did you get it? When did you suspect?"

"Relax, kid, the prizes are all yours. I never suspected anything but that Henry was a sick man. I found out because he told me."

"I can't believe it. I'm turning myself inside out to learn things, and you have people *telling* them to you. . . ."

"Sometimes, not often, something in this business can be easy. Don't knock it when it happens."

"But I was so *proud* of myself."

"Why stop now? Nothing I found out negates what you found out. What did you tell the doctors?"

"What difference does it make?"

"Are you going to pout?"

Janet said nothing.

"Okay," Ron said. "But I thought the baby was supposed to be the one on the *inside*."

Janet cracked up. When she stopped laughing, she said, "Oh, okay, but I am disappointed."

"Come on, doesn't the Professor turn all my bombshells to fizzles? Whatever I did, I didn't even do it through genius, just dumb detective luck. What did you do?"

"I called the doctors on the list and said I was Henry Pembroke's public relations adviser, and that a newspaper had been sniffing around, and they should be extra careful not to leak the results of Mr. Henry Pembroke's AIDS test. There were six on the list; five of them said they'd never heard of Mr. Henry Pembroke, and the sixth one assured me that all their tests, Mr. Pembroke's included, would remain perfectly confidential."

"Not enough for a courtroom, but not bad. Go ahead and be proud."

"What did he tell you?"

"He thinks he caught it from his late wife. A tramp of historic proportions. Mr. Jackson won't even mention her name."

"But she died eleven years ago," Janet said.

"Henry knows that."

"The average AIDS case runs ten years."

"That's the average. Obviously, some folks hold on longer. Henry figures he's on borrowed time. He had the test about three years ago, when he saw purple on himself. He's only started getting sickly over the last couple of months. He's been losing control of his emotions, too. He says he thinks that's why he made such a big stink over the bird mystery. He's happy to know they're back."

"They're *back*?"

"Oh, yeah. That was *my* big discovery for the day. They're just . . . back. I took Henry out to show him. That's where we talked, and he told me about his illness."

"The poor man."

"I agree. Maybe we can set his mind at rest, at least."

"I hope so."

"Did you talk to Chip today?"

"Nope. Didn't catch up to him. He took off in the Lincoln somewhere, maybe business, maybe just to get away from me. And the FBI. And the press."

Ron put the key in the ignition. "Come on," he said. "Let's go buy some groceries."

They found a big supermarket in a shopping center not too far from the Pembroke estate.

Ron pushed the wagon, and got goo-goo-eyed over every baby he saw. Janet smiled.

Because of the ethnic diversity of Harville, they were able to get most of the stuff the Professor (and Ron) liked to nosh on when they raided the refrigerator.

In the deli department, they picked up some black olives,

an oblong sausage called *soprassata*, and a hard ball of sharp provolone. Janet referred to this as the cholesterol special. The bakery had loaves of crusty Italian bread, judged by Ron to be superior to anything available back home in Sparta. "We'd better watch it," he said, "or the Professor will want to move here."

In the vegetable aisle, Janet pointed out a big bulb of fresh fennel, which the Professor liked to eat with a simple dressing of olive oil and vinegar, salt and pepper. The old man always managed to dip and eat the licorice-tasting stalks without spilling a drop. Janet pointed out to Ron that he lacked this skill.

"I know," he said ruefully. "And yet it *tastes* so good. I think you need to have Italian blood to do it right. Maybe we could buy me a bib."

"Ha, ha."

"We might as well get used to people in bibs."

They pushed along the aisles, picking up less exotic foods and what stores are pleased to call "health and beauty aids." When they came to the first frozen-food aisle, Ron said, "Hey, let's get some ice cream."

"I thought," Janet said, "the baby was supposed to be the one on the *inside*."

"Indulge me. When I'm a father, I'll grow up, I promise. What have we got here?"

"I see you're looking at Chip's Creamery Ice Cream."

"Yeah, it's like my version of 'Be True to Your School.' Also, everybody tells me how great it is, and I'm curious. Now let's see . . . vanilla, chocolate, double Dutch chocolate with chocolate-covered almonds, fudge brownie, fudge ripple—do you detect a trend here?—Swiss chocolate, chocolate cookie, maple walnut. At last . . . boysenberry, strawberry, peach melba, orange sorbet."

He looked up. "No grape," he said.

"Whoever heard of grape ice cream?"

"No grape sorbet, either."

"I don't think I've ever seen that. Didn't you say Chip makes a big deal of no artificial ingredients?"

"Yeah. Says so right on the container."

"Okay," Janet said. "Have you ever seen a grape-flavored anything—other than grape juice, of course—that wasn't at least partially artificially flavored?"

"Now that you mention it, no."

"So Chip doesn't make grape stuff because it takes artificial flavoring."

Ron looked puzzled. "But then—"

"What's the big grape push, anyway? I thought you liked maple walnut."

"I do, but—"

"If you want grape, let's go buy some grapes. They're better for you, anyway."

"Yeah," Ron said. "I've just had grapes on the brain lately."

"Well, let's get going. I've read that it's very important for a pregnant woman to take care of her feet."

"You don't even show yet."

"Why wait till the last minute?"

Ron grinned, grabbed a pint of maple walnut and one of orange sorbet, and hustled after his wife to the checkout.

• • •

The Professor was in the sitting room off his bedroom, watching *She Wore a Yellow Ribbon* on Cinemax. Benedetti was a hard-core Western fan, and the John Ford–John Wayne cavalry trilogy was one of his favorites. As usual, when he decided to leave his easel, he had shaved and dressed in a clean shirt and suit, including jacket and tie. He was perched on the edge of his chair, taking in the film.

"Sorry to interrupt, *Maestro*."

"'Never apologize,'" the old man quoted, "'it's a sign of weakness.'" He laughed.

"Well, you seem pretty chipper today."

"I have had a fruitful day. I have learned that Mrs. Everson, the housekeeper here, is a charming woman, and considerate to a guest."

Ron shrugged. "She'll be needing a new job, and her previous employer can't exactly give her a reference."

"You seem to have developed an alarming streak of cynicism, *amico*. It doesn't become you. Grace and dignity and beauty can be entities in themselves. Not everyone saves these things for a chance at personal gain."

Ron should have seen that coming. Benedetti was a connoisseur of "mature beauty," and if he weren't so busy studying and fighting evil, he might have campaigned vigorously for the more widespread appreciation of women over forty-five.

"*Maestro*, when we were in the woods the other day, on the way to Omega House, what did we smell?"

"Grape. Like candy. Very strong."

"That's what I thought." Ron wondered whether it was worth going into, then decided against it. He'd take a hint from Janet and make a couple of phone calls tomorrow.

"You said a very fruitful day," Ron said. "What else did you pluck?"

The old man looked disapproval at Ron, but let it pass. "I believe I have solved the case," he said.

"Oh."

Janet walked in.

"The Professor has solved the case," Ron told her.

"Oh," she said.

"I *believe* I have solved it. I must check my evidence. And the precise motive eludes me. But the core of it, I am convinced I have seen."

Ron shook his head. "*Maestro*, I'm usually panting along behind you somewhere, but this time, I haven't seen a thing."

"You still have time. There are some matters that mystify me even now. The matter of the birds, for instance."

"Their being gone or their being back?"

"Their being gone. They are back because their absence has served its purpose and is no longer necessary to the plan. As to the mechanism by which they were made to vanish, I am still completely in the dark."

"If you remember, *Maestro*, that was what we were brought down here to figure out."

"Time has made the question . . . not irrelevant, but, let us say, secondary." He rubbed his jaw. "Not that it still doesn't need to be answered."

"But the disappearing birds are still part of the case. The kidnapping and all."

"The murder. Yes, I am certain of it."

On the screen, Ben Johnson caught up with John Wayne with the message from the Yankee War Department, and the movie was more or less over. Benedetti switched off the TV and said, "Excellent film, as always. 'I am a Christian!'" He laughed. "But, my children, you must tell me about your day. Perhaps you have found the other end of a string, that we may tie up the loose ends."

"Janet did the major detective work today, *Maestro*. Followed up a hunch and it paid off."

"Indeed, Doctor. And what did you learn?"

Janet told him what she'd found out.

Benedetti raised his head, taking a deep breath and closing his eyes while he did.

There was a tense silence for a few moments, then, "Excellent. Truly excellent. This fits my theory perfectly. It must be confirmed, of course—"

"All taken care of, *Maestro*. Henry told me so, himself."

"I believe the case is all but solved—all except for the problem of those accursed birds. You must excuse me; I must think."

Back to the old drawing board, Ron thought. Or painting board, as the case may be.

"*Maestro*," Ron said, "wait a second."

"Yes?" Benedetti was impatient.

"Before you go, can I have a little hint? I might as well be doing some thinking, too."

"No hints."

It was foolish, but Ron felt hurt.

"They are not necessary. You must only remember what I have taught you."

"Very well, *Maestro*." Ron was meek. He could tease the old man, and often did, but not at a time like this, not when Benedetti's voice got that deadly edge to it.

"Remember the very first thing I said I would require of you?"

"I had to learn to speak Italian."

"No, after that. Relating to the actual *work*."

"To watch and listen."

"Precisely. And, in this case, the second is greater than the first."

"Thank you," Ron said.

Just then, the housekeeper bustled in. She was obviously agitated, but she had a smile for the old man, anyway.

"Chief Viretsky is here. He'd like to see you all."

They went downstairs. The chief was more agitated than Mrs. Everson.

"I cut across the estate on my way to the highway. Figured you might want to be in on this."

"In on what, Chief Viretsky?" Benedetti asked.

"Got a buzz from Precton, two towns over. Seems that Chip Pembroke just got blown to bits."

E i g h t

Sandy had finally gotten the bill from NEFF straightened out this morning. Well, not straightened out, exactly, but at least taken off her shoulders. Mr. Pembroke—Chip—told her he'd take care of it, and Sandy didn't have to worry about it anymore.

Then he asked her to join him for lunch.

She was so shocked she gawked at him. She saw a scared look come over his face.

"Oh. I'm out of line. . . . I'm sorry, Sandy—Miss Jovanka, really. . . . I promise it'll never happen again—"

"It's all right, Mr. Pembroke, really."

"That's good of you, Sandy. I don't know what came over me, I just—"

Sandy decided she'd better take charge of this before it got too difficult. "No, really. I'd love to have lunch with you. Really."

His smile was just like a little boy's.

"You would?"

"Uh-huh."

"Okay," Chip said. "We'll go somewhere really nice." He went into his office, and came out a few minutes later.

"I made reservations at the Continental, in Precton. Is that all right?"

"Sure, it's fine. But Precton's a half-hour drive. We'll never have time to eat and get me back here on time."

"Your boss gives you special permission to take a long lunch."

Sandy giggled. "Well, that's okay, then."

They went in his car. Of *course* they went in his car. Her car was a dumb old little Toyota Cressida with the tailpipe held up by a coat hanger until she could afford to go to a muffler shop.

She giggled. "I'm riding a Lincoln to the Continental."

"I'm sorry I picked a place so far away," Chip said. "It's just that in Precton, there'll be a slightly less chance of being recognized and hounded. I . . . I don't think I could handle gossip right now, on top of everything else."

"Oh. Oh, of course, Mr. Pembroke. I know about the reporters. I've had a few camped on my doorstep, yelling questions at me. But I haven't really said anything." She had, of course, posed for pictures, but there couldn't be anything wrong with that.

"Call me Chip."

"Chip. No, no gossip. You've been through an awful lot. It must have been horrible. Everybody who works at the shop is awfully sorry about what happened. . . ."

"I know. And I appreciate it. But it does make you happy to be alive, you know? And it makes you want to think."

"Think?" Sandy said.

"About what's important. About what you might be missing. My uncle was incredibly rich. Incredibly. And all he had to make him happy was a bunch of cats with no tails."

"I think they're sweet."

"I guess so, but that's not the point. He was in his seventies, and he'd had most of his chances to do and be what he wanted to be."

"He was a very great man, my mom says."

"Sure, but what happened to him could happen to anybody."

"Not anybody," she pointed out. "Most people couldn't pay ten thousand dollars, let alone a million."

A pained look crossed Chip's face. Sandy was instantly sorry. "Oh, I didn't mean that. You're right, you're right, horrible things can happen to anybody."

"It's okay, honey."

Sandy felt a little thrill. He had called her "honey." God must have been listening, there at the cemetery.

"It's true, about terrible things happening to anyone, but it wasn't what I meant. I meant that the same things that made my Uncle Clyde a target can also make me a target."

"Don't say that."

"I can't run from the truth, Sandy. The trouble is, I'm just not ready to go. I've got so much to do. My dad's not a young man anymore, and Harry Swantek won't be able to do it alone, even with the block of stock my uncle left him."

"I heard about that."

"Well, Harry deserves it. But Pembroke Industries needs a Pembroke involved. It took me a long time to prove I'm a good businessman, but I *am*.

"And there's so much to do. The smoke scrubber is just the beginning. Environmental technology is a field without limits. Clean luxury! It's what America wants. We've got a jump on the rest of the country—the rest of the world—and I want to keep running with it, and stay ahead. I'm sure Harry will agree with me."

"He's got to!" Sandy was excited. "This is the only planet we've got!"

Chip smiled at her. "Hold that thought. It can be a beautiful place, too. A little lonely, maybe, but beautiful."

At the same time Sandy's brain was whirling, it was also clicking like a taxi meter. He had called her "honey." He confessed to being lonely. And, part three, the Continental Restaurant was attached to a Holiday Inn. One of the nicer ones around.

The Continental was busy, but not crowded. They got a quiet table, looked at the menu, and ordered. Or, rather, Sandy told Chip to order for her. He said a bunch of French stuff to the waiter. When it came, it turned out to be fish with some kind of sauce, but it wasn't icky the way fish usually was, and there was white wine and little tiny potatoes and some asparagus. She ate it up, and they talked.

Chip started by telling her he appreciated what a good job she'd done for the company, and how staunch she had been during the kidnapping crisis, staying out of touch with people and putting up with all the tension.

She took a sip of wine. "It was nothing compared to *your* tension." She made a face. "Nobody's ever called me 'staunch' before."

"Pretty romantic, huh?" He seemed angry with himself. Romantic.

"Actually, I kind of like it," she said.

"Thanks."

Then he asked her about herself, and she told him, and then she asked him to tell her about himself.

"Oh, it's old stuff," he said.

"No, that's what this is all about, right? I mean, I know you as a boss, as a 'Pembroke.' I want to get to know you as a person."

"I think that's a pretty good idea. Okay. My real name is Humbert. After my great-grandfather, who founded the family fortune. Right there, I entered life with a strike against me."

Chip went on to tell her how he'd been a shy kid with no choice but to have the whole town notice everything he did. And then with his mother going wild—she was a woman who had a Reputation and really lived up to it, Sandy reflected—the giggling and finger-pointing were occasions of agony for him. He couldn't do anything, not even run away, because Pembrokes didn't do that.

"And I spent most of my life running away. Boarding school, college, New York. My father wanted me to come into the business, but I didn't. I had to prove myself to myself with the ice-cream business, first."

"You didn't run away the other night." Sandy reached across the table and took his hand. "It didn't work out, but it wasn't your fault. You did all you could. You didn't run away."

He put his other hand on top of hers. "No, I didn't. And I'm never going to run away from anything else, either."

"Like what?"

His voice was very soft. "Like you."

"That's a good idea."

"I wish I'd had the guts to tell you sooner how I feel about you."

"How *do* you feel about me?"

"Oh, God, I wish I had the words. I wish you could read my mind. I wish we could . . . right now . . ."

Sandy said, "Let's."

• • •

It was wonderful. The whole thing was wonderful. He'd checked into the hotel using his platinum American Express card. With *his own name on it.* So this wasn't going to be a sneaking-around kind of thing. This was going to be for real. And if it didn't end up at the altar (or a courthouse, or a justice of the peace), Sandy knew it wasn't going to be her fault.

The rest of it was pretty wonderful, too. Chip had been nervous and shy, and Sandy had sort of had to jump-start him a little, but after that, he'd been fine. Both times. He *needed* her so much. Sandy would be good for him, she knew it. And he'd be good for her.

A while later, lying together, Chip said, "Oh, goddammit."

"What's wrong?"

"Distribution contracts with FreezLines. I've got to sign them and get them in the mail this afternoon."

"Oh." Sandy sighed. "Back to the office, huh? I'll try not to glow or anything where anybody can see me, Chip."

"What the hell," he told her. "Glow all you want. I want to tell the world about you. But we don't have to go back to the office. I took them home last night to check them over, take my mind off things, you know. I stuck them under the driver's seat in the car."

"Then we just have to get them."

Chip groaned. "But it's so nice, just lying here."

"I'll get them."

"I don't want to put you through the trouble, either."

"No trouble. Just think of me, and I'll be back before you know it."

"The combination is in my pants pocket."

"I've got it." Sandy didn't bother with underwear, just slipped her dress on over her head and stepped into her shoes. She bent over the bed and kissed Chip.

"Have a nice trip," he said, smiling up at her.

She smiled back. "Give me a warm welcome when I come back."

The car was down at the bottom of the stairs. Sandy punched the numbers on the little slip of paper into the lock, then opened the door.

There was a sheet of yellow flame. She never heard the noise.

"Chief," Ron Gentry said, "I think you got it slightly wrong."

"What do you mean?"

They had left the highway and followed the smoke and lines of police cars and fire trucks to the parking lot of a Holiday Inn. Viretsky had had to use his credentials at least fifteen times to get this close. Right now, they were outside a ring of fire trucks surrounding the remains of what sure as hell looked like one of the Pembrokes' fleet of Lincolns.

"Chip Pembroke is over there," Gentry said. "In a Mylar blanket. Not dead."

Viretsky looked. It certainly was Chip Pembroke, sobbing and hysterical, but very much alive. It was time to find out what was going on around here.

Viretsky gave up trying to find a decent place to park. He just stopped his car and said, "Okay, everybody out."

A fat, bald little guy who looked like Nikita Khrushchev quickly waddled over to him.

The bald guy pulled his right hand out of the pocket of his fur-collared leather jacket, shook Viretsky's hand, and said, "Hi, Chet, looks like your little problem is my little problem, too." He jerked his chins at Benedetti and his assistants. "Ahh, who are these nice folks?"

"Let me introduce you. Chief Roy Abruzzi of Precton, this is Professor Niccolo Benedetti, and his assistants, Ron Gentry and Janet Higgins."

Abruzzi pumped the Professor's hand. "Benedetti, huh? *Buon giorno, paesano.*"

"Buon giorno a lei stesso."

"Professor? What, from Penn State?"

If Viretsky hadn't known Abruzzi was a tough, skilled, New York City trained cop, he would have been convinced the man was an asshole. As it was, Viretsky found him extremely embarrassing.

"Professor Benedetti," Viretsky interjected, "is a world-famous philosopher and criminologist." Viretsky darted a glance at Benedetti. Putting "philosopher" first seemed to have appeased the old man.

"What's going on, Roy? My dispatcher had it that Chip Pembroke was killed."

"Nah, it was a girl. His secretary." Abruzzi looked at his notebook. "Alexandra June Jovanka, of Harville."

"I know her."

"You wouldn't now," Abruzzi said brightly. "We're gonna have to make this official from baby footprints. We found a whole foot, so far."

Viretsky was studying the smoldering car. "What was it?"

"Two, three sticks of dynamite is my guess. Simple goddamn bomb, a tenth grader could do it if he got the dynamite. Magnet stuck under the driver's seat doorsill, little wire stuck to the door sets it off when the door is opened. Could be planted in fifteen seconds. Could have been planted days ago, and just *armed* in two seconds."

"What—" Janet Higgins's voice was a little strained, but it was smooth again on the second try. "What were they doing here, Chief Abruzzi?"

Abruzzi shrugged. "My guess is the usual. You know, when a boss and a secretary take a hotel room with no luggage in another town in the middle of the afternoon."

"A liaison," Benedetti said.

Abruzzi smiled Khrushchev's avuncular smile. "Yeah. I

like that. They'd been liaisoning up there for a couple of hours when Pembroke apparently thought of something he needed from the car, and the girl said she'd go get it. I think. He ain't been too coherent, if you know what I mean."

Ron Gentry said, "He's had a tough week."

Abruzzi put his hand over his mouth. "Don't make me laugh, will ya? Get my picture in the paper laughing at a time like this, I get the city council on my ass again."

It occurred to Viretsky that if Abruzzi found this all so goddamn amusing, he could have the whole case.

"Can we talk to him?"

"Sure. Help yourself."

• • •

With the metallized Mylar held tight around him, Chip looked to Ron like a joint of meat ready for the oven. A couple of ambulance guys led Chip into the hotel manager's office and let him sit. Abruzzi ran the manager off and went to attend to his men, but not before getting a promise to be brought up-to-date when the interview was over.

"Chip?" Ron began.

Chip was staring intently at something in a dimension only he had access to. His face was very pale.

"Chip? *Chip!*"

"Huh? Oh. Ron. How did you get here?"

"Don't worry about that. I'm here. So're Janet and the Professor."

Chip looked blankly at them. "Thanks," he said.

"Chip, you've got to tell us what happened, okay?"

"I killed her."

"*You* killed her? Why?"

A little life came into Chip's face. "What do you mean, *why*?"

"You said you killed her. I want to know either why you did it, or if you didn't do it, I want to know why you *said* it."

"Well, she died because of me, didn't she? She died *instead* of me, didn't she?" He was roaring now. "If she hadn't come with me this afternoon, she'd be alive, wouldn't she? Wouldn't she?" His voice dropped to a mutter. "And I'd be dead. I'd be dead like Uncle Clyde. Somebody wants us dead, Ron. All the Pembrokes."

Chip jumped to his feet and grabbed Ron by the shoulders. "Dad! I've got to get to Dad!"

"Sit down, Chip."

"Don't you understand? They missed me, they're going to go after my father next. Let me go, dammit!"

He tried to push past Ron, knocking Ron's glasses off in the process. This posed a triple problem for Ron. Wrapping up Chip, doing it without hurting him, and not letting anyone step on his glasses.

The Professor solved it for him.

"Mr. Pembroke."

Ron wished he knew how the Professor did that. It was forceful, but it wasn't a shout. There was something in the tone that was impossible to ignore.

"Mr. Pembroke, sit down. You have nothing to worry about."

"But my father—"

"You have my word that your father is in no danger."

"But how can you know?"

"I know. You must trust me now. You must not let your re-action to the explosion destroy you as the bomb itself could not. If we are to punish whoever did this, you must gather yourself. You must help us now."

Ron started to look for his glasses, but Janet had already picked them up. She handed them to him. He blew a piece of carpet fluff off the left lens, and put them on. Then, gently and slowly, he drew the story out. Chip sobbed softly, especially when he talked about Sandy.

"She thought she was so hip, but she was really so innocent, you know?" he said, and "I told her I wasn't going to waste my life anymore," and "I think I might really have loved her; I just wanted to get close to somebody, and look at what happened. God, why didn't *I* go get the papers? The curse is on *me*. *I'm the one who's supposed to be dead!*"

Ron knelt in front of him. The weeping man put his arms around him and held on.

After a few seconds, Ron nodded to the ambulance guys. They replaced the Mylar on Chip's shoulders and led him out to the ambulance.

Ron sighed. "Looks like another night under heavy sedation for that boy."

"At least," the chief said. "He bounced back incredibly well, last time."

Janet nodded. "Surprisingly well. He seems emotionally frail, but there's strong stuff in him."

"If he survives this," Ron added, "running a major corporation will be a snap for him, as far as stress goes."

"Yes," the Professor said. "Some things can stand it, some can't. My theory of the case, for instance, cannot withstand the stress of these events."

"Theory?" Viretsky demanded.

"Yes. I had a theory of which I was quite fond. But there was no room in it for the murder of either Chip Pembroke or his secretary. Therefore, I must start over. At the source. Chief, do you have copies of the tapes from the night of Clyde Pembroke's murder?"

"They're easy enough to make."

"I should like a set. There is something I must check." The old man sighed heavily. "Perhaps, I have outlived my usefulness. When Niccolo Benedetti cannot trust his own memory, he is the next thing to dead."

T e n

The next morning, after a night spent in equal parts of listening to Chip's voice as he drew ever closer to his uncle's corpse, fending the press off the Professor, and having fitful dreams of blood and bombs and screaming birds, Ron found he couldn't breathe. In his sleep, he fought for breath, but nothing came into his lungs. With a sudden effort, he sat up in bed.

"*RRRRRaaaaaarrrrrr!*" Nimrod said as he sailed across the room. He ran around madly for a half-minute or so, while Ron filled his lungs. Then the kitten started to claw his way determinedly back to bed.

Ron picked up Nimrod by the scruff of his neck, at which point, of course, following universal cat instinct, the kitten went limp, and looked like the cutest, most harmless, most innocent thing in the world.

"You," Ron said, "are a problem. Should I pet you or break your neck?"

"*Mrowr,*" Nimrod said.

Ron decided to pet him. "Been too much violence around here already," he said.

Janet woke up. She looked up with an expression that combined sleepiness and myopia. "What time is it?"

"Seven-thirty."

"Oh. After last night, I didn't think you'd get up so early."

"Wasn't my idea. Nimrod decided to see how long I could go without oxygen."

"Huh?"

"While I was sleeping, he lay down across my face." Ron wiggled his eyebrows like Groucho Marx. "Which reminds me of a story so dirty, I'm ashamed to think of it myself."

"Tell me."

"No."

"Ro-on."

"Later. Are you up, or should I take the Red Menace out of here so you can get some more sleep? I don't dare try. God knows what he'll do to me next time."

"I'm up."

"Good. Let's see if we can arrange for breakfast and the Yellow Pages. The Professor said he was going back to the beginning. I'm going back to *before* the beginning."

"What do you mean?"

"I am finding out about grapes."

• • •

He began his research with breakfast. The housekeeper was more than glad to drown her concerns over poor Chip in work, and she whipped up a breakfast of monumental proportions. There was bacon and scrambled eggs and home fries and biscuits, orange juice and coffee. Ron put gobs of grape jam on the biscuits and on the eggs.

"I'll never get used to your doing that," Janet said, as he brought a yellow-and-purple forkful to his mouth.

"Oh, I never knew it bothered you."

"It doesn't *bother* me in the sense that it grosses me out. It just seems so *strange*."

"It's very simple, dear. I hate eggs, but I love jam. This way, I don't have to answer why I didn't eat the eggs when someone is nice enough to make them for me."

"I know, but still . . ."

"One of these days, I'll make you a peanut-butter-and-tomato sandwich."

"That *does* gross me out."

"It did me, too, when I first heard about it. Tried it on a dare. It's terrific."

"I'll take your word for it. How'd it go in the Yellow Pages?"

"Great. There's a place just outside Scranton. Flavor Formulas. I think I'll go in person."

"Won't they tell you on the phone?"

"I don't know. They're not open yet. They probably would. I just want to get the hell out of Harville for a little while, you know?"

"Sure."

• • •

The Pembroke-centered crime wave had seriously depleted the supply of Lincolns in the Pembroke fleet. Ron and Janet rode in the small car they'd used the other day.

"You're worried, aren't you?" Janet asked after a while.

"Worried?"

"About the Professor."

"Yeah. A little. Because he's worried about himself. He's been preaching humility to me for years, but this case is the first time he's ever actually shown me any. It's not supposed to be like that. Benedetti is supposed to be able to figure out anything, and lead me to figure it out, too."

"Take it as a compliment," Janet suggested.

"That the old man is losing his confidence?"

"No, Ron. That the old man is letting you see that he's not always as confident as he lets on. That as brilliant as he is, he's human."

"He's got a lot of nerve, turning human all of a sudden. I've spent a lot of my life since college depending on him."

"You're about to be a father, Ron."

"Yeah?"

"We're going to have a child who'll think you are the

208 • William L. DeAndrea

biggest, strongest, wisest, smartest being in the universe. You'll have all the answers, and be able to fix all the problems. And then one day, you won't, and you'll have to let the kid in on the secret—that you're only human, after all.

"Of course," she went on, "even if a situation never does come up that you can't handle, you'll still have to get the message across. A kid has to learn it; can't grow up otherwise."

"You mean—"

"I think the Professor's finally about to give you your diploma, dear."

"Doesn't matter much if we don't break the case." Ron's voice was gruff, but Janet could see he was touched. She just hoped she was right.

• • •

Flavor Formulas, Inc., was in a low, brick building, about the size and appearance of an elementary school built for baby-boomers in the 1950s. Inside, they were welcomed and shown to a lab. There, they met Cathy Sang, a Chinese-American woman about Janet's age and half her size. Cathy wore a lab coat over a yellow cowl-neck sweater and a plaid skirt.

"How may I help you?" she asked.

"I'm a private investigator, licensed in New York." Ron showed her his ID. "I'm working on a case that involves someone encountering a strong grape smell, like artificial grape flavoring. Like in Kool-Aid or soda."

"When you said you were a private investigator, I thought, Oh, how exciting."

"Just routine," Ron said.

He always did that, no matter what he was working on. It was as if he had to say it or lose his license. People *wanted* a little excitement in their lives, Janet would tell him, but it never did any good.

Cathy Sang smiled. It transformed her face. "So is grape flavoring," she told him. "As you might guess, grape is one of our most popular products. What would you like to know?"

"Anything you can tell me."

"Well, we make several kinds, different shades and colors of taste, but they all have the same basic ingredient. Methyl anthranilate."

"Would you spell that, please?"

Ron wrote it down. Janet was surprised. He hardly ever used a notebook.

"Is there any reason you'd be likely to smell this stuff in the woods?"

"In the woods? No. Unless someone had spilled a soda, I suppose."

"Mmmm. How about at an airport?"

Cathy Sang brightened. "Oh, yes. You'd be quite likely to smell methyl anthranilate at an airport. Especially lately. Especially at airports by the sea."

Ron's eyes widened behind his glasses. "I would?"

The chemist nodded, smiling brightly.

"Because of the birds," she said.

E l e v e n

Leaving the building, they were both excited, but Ron was positively trembling. He fumbled in his pocket and handed Janet the keys.

"You drive," he said. "I'd crack us up. Besides, I have to think this out."

"But this means—"

"I know what it means." He got in the car. Janet buckled herself in and started the motor.

About three miles down the road, Ron said, "I'm sorry. God knows why I'm snapping at you. It's just what this all implies is so crazy, I'm not much better than a lunatic."

"But now we know—"

"All we know," Ron went on, not realizing he'd cut Janet off again, "is that Chip is almost certainly the one behind the disappearance of the birds. We don't know why. We sure as hell know he didn't kill his uncle, and he didn't booby-trap his own car and kill off his secretary. Even the Professor said there was no reason to do that."

They drove on for a while in a tense silence. Once, Ron hit the padded dashboard three times, hard, with his fist.

Nearing the entrance to the Pembroke estate, he said, "The Professor told me to listen. Listen to what?"

"He also was telling you to remember what you've heard." Janet shrugged. "Of course, he's given up that theory."

"I still want to know what he's spotted. Maybe it can fit in with this somehow."

Janet made the turn up the gravel drive, going perhaps a little too fast. She eased up on the accelerator slightly. "Well," she said, "what has the Professor been listening to?"

At least, she tried to say it. The small car bounced so much on the gravel that she had trouble understanding herself.

Ron looked like a man who'd just stepped on a stingray. His eyes opened so wide she could see pink around them.

"*Of course!*" he yelled. A few seconds later, he said, "*Now* there's a reason, dammit."

A few more seconds after that, he said, "Stop the car."

"What?"

"Stop the car right now. I've got to do something."

Dutifully, Janet pulled over to the side of the drive and braked gently to a stop.

"Out of the car," Ron said. He was already clambering out himself. Janet unbuckled her seat belt and came around the car to meet Ron.

He put his arms around her, bent her backward, and kissed her in a way she had never previously been kissed with shoes on.

"What was that about?" she demanded when she'd caught her breath. "Not that I mind, but what was that about?"

"It was about the end of the case. You solved it."

"I did?"

Janet didn't know whether to be pleased or angry. Benedetti was always telling her that she had an instinct that took her straight to the key element of an investigation, and that was gratifying. The fact that she herself never recognized when she was doing it was infuriating. Now the same thing was happening with Ron.

"You drive now," she said. "I want to think."

Ron drove on. Fast, faster than she'd been going. She asked him to slow down.

He grinned at her. She started to yell, and then she got it.

"The tape," she said.

Ron slowed down.

• • •

When they got to Alpha House, Ron ran upstairs to Benedetti's room. Janet would have been ahead of him, if it weren't for her heels. She caught up to him as he was knocking on the door.

"*Maestro*," he called, "it's us. We've got something. We've got *everything*."

"A moment, *amico, per favore*."

"He's putting his shirt on," Ron murmured. "Just me, he would see in his undershirt."

Benedetti was adjusting his bow tie as he opened the door. He nodded. "Such excitement on your faces. If I heard you correctly, you have fulfilled the universal desire."

"I don't get it, *Maestro*."

"He means we've got everything," Janet said. To the old man, she said, "We think so. Your theory was ri—"

"*Lentamente*. Slowly. You have learned something today, and from this, you conclude you have reasoned out the case."

"Exactly," Ron said.

"I ask the same privilege. I would like to know what you have learned. Perhaps I can reach the same conclusion."

It was only fair; Janet was so pleased to be out of the dark at this stage of a case, she'd forgotten that neither she nor Ron would be anywhere near a solution without the old man's hint.

Ron, of course, had launched into the explanation without a second thought. By the time Janet tuned back in, he had just told Benedetti about the chemist's remark about airports and birds.

"... come to find out, *Maestro*," he was saying, "methyl anthranilate tastes like grape to us—"

Benedetti made a face. "Remotely."

Ron grinned. "At least it passes for grape. To a human.

"To a bird, though, it's incredibly nasty stuff. When it hits their skin or eyes or mucous membranes, it burns the way hot pepper burns us."

"Ah," Benedetti said. "You smelled grape in the birdless wood."

"Yes, sir."

"And I chided you. I ascribed it to the presence on the estate of an ice-cream factory."

"It made sense. You weren't the one who heard the spiel about 'all-natural ingredients.' I was. And I was also the one who was out in the woods when they really were cooking up a flavor, and I didn't smell anything."

"Thank you, *amico*. Your words are some consolation. Nevertheless, I have been a fool. It shall not happen again."

"I never would have done a thing about it, if I hadn't had grape on the brain. See, they've begun spraying the stuff at airports where birds are a problem. It keeps them away, reduces accidents, and does no permanent damage to the birds. It was written up in a trade journal called *F&F*—stands for 'flavors and fragrances,' I think."

"We must ask about their subscription list. See to it, won't you, *amico*? Of course, the thing is quite obvious now. By the time you are done calling, I shall have the details worked out. And perhaps I will think of what to do with our knowledge."

While Ron went to the other room to call, and the Professor settled in an armchair to think, Janet looked at Benedetti's latest canvas. It seemed to be finished, but it wasn't signed.

The shape that had resembled a peace symbol before was still there, in the center of the painting, but dividing each line of red was a shaft of black. Around the rim of the circle, fierce-looking white triangles, like fangs, seemed to close in on it. The whole affair was framed in a bright, blood red. It looked like some nightmare cavern, or the monstrous organ of a perverted fantasy.

Janet, you relentless shrink, cut it out, she told herself.

Ron came back, nodding. "Chip's Creamery is a subscriber to *F&F*, and has been since well before the methyl anthranilate article came out."

"*Va bene.*" The Professor rose to his feet. "This has been a case, on a small scale, remarkable in its evil," he said. "And damage is still to be done. My friends, I have been accustomed to calling the tune. As we have arrived at the solution in this instance more or less together, I feel it only fitting that this time we confer about what we are to do."

"What we are to do?" Janet echoed. "We get Viretsky over here and fill him in on this." She looked at the frowning faces of her husband and the Professor. "Don't we?"

"That," the old man said, "is what we must discuss." He turned to the canvas and rubbed his chin. "But wait. With your indulgence, there is something I must do first."

He took off his tweed jacket and draped it over a chair. Then he picked up his palette and a tube of blue acrylic. He squeezed a dab of blue onto the palette, then mixed it with red and white already there until he had a light purple color, not quite pastel. This he swirled across the canvas, like a thin vapor. Then, using the same color, he painted the stylized "B" in the corner.

He put down the palette and put his jacket back on. "There," he said. "That is finished. Now let us decide how to put an end to this."

T w e l v e

Much to Chip's surprise, it was Ron Gentry, in the little Dodge, who picked him up at the hospital. It had been a restful two days, but it was time to get on with life.

"It's good to see you, Ron," Chip said. "But I was expecting Jackson."

"He's with your father."

"My father? Is something wrong?"

"Well, he's kind of worn out, but he's showing the flag for you. There's a memorial service for Sandy today."

"Oh, God. Poor Sandy. I should be there." Chip's face crumpled.

"They'll understand."

"I'm going to make sure Sandy's mother is taken care of. I swear it."

"That's good. Need any help?"

"No, I can make it. I'm okay physically. It's emotions that keep getting me in here."

"You've had some week."

There was something strange about Ron's voice. "Is that supposed to be *funny*, for God's sake?" Chip demanded.

"No, I don't think it's funny."

"Good."

That didn't come off right, Chip decided. He was much better off with Gentry on his side. "Look, I'm really sorry about that. I know it's been tough on you, too."

"I'm used to it."

"I know you and the Professor have done your best."

"Maybe."

"Where are you going?"

"I'm taking a scenic route."

"But that's *Punchy's*!"

"Uh-huh." Ron pulled into the parking lot and stopped. He waited a few minutes, and drove on to the next stop the tape said Chip had made the night he was driving around with a million dollars in the car.

"Ron, this really isn't funny."

"I agree."

The next stop. And the next.

"Stop the car!"

"When the time comes."

"Cut it out right now, you sick son of a bitch."

"Shut up," Ron said calmly.

Chip tried to jump him, to grab the steering wheel, but Gentry had anticipated the move. He shot out his right arm and caught Chip under the chin with the heel of his hand. The blow stunned Chip. He subsided.

"You're going to suffer for this," he hissed, after another mile.

"Try it again," Ron invited.

"No, thanks. I'm saving you for later."

"Yeah? Well, I'm taking care of you right now."

He turned off the road, and began bouncing up the drive past the old main gate.

"Talk to me," Gentry said, his voice juddering from the bouncing of the car.

"Go to hell," Chip juddered back.

"More! Call me a bastard!"

"I'll call you every name in the book! What the hell do you think you're doing?"

Gentry ignored the question. "There's the old gatehouse. We should have known it was you when nobody went for the million. You didn't give a damn about a measly million. You were playing for the whole thing."

"You're crazy!"

Gentry stopped the car just beyond the stake-and-ribbon outlines of the Lincoln Town Car and the Samurai.

"Now you get out. Don't try to run, the woods are staked out. Don't try to jump me, or I swear I'll cripple you."

Chip worked his sore jaw. After a moment, he got out of the car.

"I assume you had a gun on your uncle. Either that, or you'd tied him up already. Friday night. The night you kidnapped him."

"Rave on."

"Yeah. Inside the barn."

Chip stepped inside. There, by the light of a kerosene lantern, he saw a man in a chair in the middle of the barn with his head thrown back, and a small cat perched on top.

For a second, Chip froze. Then he took another look.

"Of all the cheap, tasteless— You can get off that chair, Professor Benedetti."

"With pleasure," the Professor said. He gently removed the cat from his head—it was the same cat, Chip suspected—and cradled it in his arm.

"What is going on here?" Chip demanded.

"We are fulfilling our commission," the old man told him. "Your father engaged us to find the killer of his brother, no matter what the consequences, and we have done so. How sad for Miss Jovanka we failed to do so sooner."

Chip spat on the dirt floor.

"You will oblige us by answering a few questions," Benedetti said. "Take a seat."

He gestured to the chair. They looked so grim, the jerks. Chip wasn't worried. He sat.

"Did you have to screw her?" Ron said.

Chip Pembroke looked up at him. The slightest suggestion

of a grin played at the corners of his lips. "We were in love,"
he replied.

"Yeah, love. I realize, by your standards, you had to kill
her. But you could have set that bomb trick up anywhere—
at the office, outside the restaurant—and sent her out for
the stuff. She'd be just as dead, and you'd look just as innocent. Why did you have to use her like that first?"

"You're incredibly insulting, you know that?"

"Maybe God will give me a pimple on my tongue. I am
glad to inform you that she got you, anyway, Chip. It was
that invoice she wanted to talk about that Saturday morning, the one she didn't understand. I've checked it out. It
was from a flavoring company, one you did a lot of business
with. That part was no big deal.

"But the invoice was for *artificial grape flavoring*. And
Sandy knew you never used anything artificial. She must
have wondered if the whole thing was a mistake. Especially
in such quantities—yeah, I've been on the phone to the sup-
plier, too."

"And they told you my business practices? Shame on
them."

"Shame on me, I told them a lie."

Ron turned his back on Chip. It was a dare.

But Chip sat tight. Still with his back turned, Ron went
on. "There was no mistake. You were filling the forest with
methyl anthranilate."

Benedetti chuckled. "That made him flinch."

"You were driving the birds from the forest, Chip. You
were playing mind games with your father and your uncle."

"Indeed," Benedetti said. "I am looking forward to my
hour alone with you—after you have been arrested and locked
safely away, of course. It will be interesting to explore the *reasons* for your terror campaign. Was it simple malice? Or were
the missing birds and the dead cat—and how many stray cats

did you kill before your uncle stumbled upon one, I wonder?—steps in a malignant campaign to convince the twins, as it ultimately did, that someone was persecuting them? That would certainly lend credence to the idea you so carefully planted and nurtured—that a gang of implacable kidnappers was out to hurt the Pembrokes in every way possible. This was a gang so confident they sent ransom notes before the kidnapping; so shadowy, we never got a glimpse of them.

"Why, they had the confidence of madness. Could they not order the forces of nature so as to make the birds disappear? Were they not ruthless enough to murder innocent cats on the virtual doorstep of the area's best-known and most powerful cat lover?

"And no wonder we never found a trace of them, for they didn't exist."

"There's another possibility, *Maestro*," Ron said.

"Yes, *amico*?"

"He might have played his little stunts, and made bad blood between his father and his uncle, to hold up production on the smoke scrubber."

"Why? The smoke scrubber would only enrich Pembroke Industries. Full control of that is the prize he sought, eh?"

Chip sneered at Ron. "Your turn. This is fascinating."

"It is," Ron said, "in its own sick way. You wanted to delay the smoke scrubber because you *knew* the EPA was hot to have the thing in production. They'd send somebody to get to the bottom of it, somebody good."

"And, gosh," Chip sneered, "I got me the World-Famous Professor Benedetti."

"That must have just made your day, too," Ron said. "Because in your mind, you're not the pathetic little vicious shithead you are in real life, you're an undiscovered *genius*, aren't you, who should be running the vast industrial empire you've grown up wanting instead of a small regional ice-cream company. Those two old fogies had no business standing in your way. Your father was a cuckold who'd let your tramp of a mother give him AIDS, and your uncle was a fool who wasted his affection on cats who didn't even have tails. Right?"

Nimrod, still in Benedetti's arms, said *"Mrowr!"* Ron wondered if the old man had pinched him.

In any case, the timing was perfect. Chip's glance shot to the cat much more quickly than that of a man as calm as he was pretending to be.

"The really pathetic thing about you was that you did all this in jealousy of Harry Swantek."

"Me? Jealous of that jumped-up jock? Don't make me laugh, Gentry."

"Yeah, jealous of that jumped-up jock. That got to you, didn't it? Because Swantek had started with nothing and gotten with hard work what you wanted handed to you on a silver platter. You would inherit the family business in time, or a goodly portion of it—your father's half. But you couldn't count on Clyde's anymore, could you? Clyde always liked Harry; he'd already arranged to leave him a block of stock in his will. I don't know if you knew that, but you damn well suspected it. The question was, would he get enough influence over your uncle, enough stock in the will, to be a nuisance to you when you took over? You couldn't risk it.

"I've got to commend you for not just killing Swantek. That would have been messy—your motive might have been uncovered. And, besides, he's very good at what he does. You didn't mind having him running the plant and making you *money*, you just didn't want him to have the power. The power was going to be all yours, right, Chip? Power's what this whole thing is all about, isn't it? Power over the business, power over the beloved Pembroke brothers, power over the World-Famous Niccolo Benedetti"—Ron grinned sourly—

"and his entourage, power over the town, and power over poor Sandy Jovanka. Body and mind. Life and death."

Chip laced his fingers behind his head and leaned back in the chair. "Even if everything you say is true, even if I *admit* spraying grape flavoring in that section of woods and bashing a few stray cats—"

"Do you?"

He grinned. "Sure. I admit it, at least here to you. Why the hell not? It was good for a few laughs. But as I was saying, even if all that is true, you don't have any evidence. Not one single goddam shred of evidence."

"Oh," the Professor said in a silken voice, "but we do."

• • •

For the first time since they'd arrived at the big old barn, Benedetti came around so that Chip could see him. The old man smiled grimly at Chip and said nothing. Chip's hands came loose from behind his head. The front legs of the chair hit the ground, and the smile left his face. He met the Professor's gaze in silence for a few seconds. Ron thought he saw him starting to sweat.

"Bullshit," Chip said at last. "This is a bluff."

"A bluff?" The Professor put a hand to his heart. "You wound me, Chip. I am the World-Famous Niccolo Benedetti, for whose presence here you are directly responsible. Would you want to match wits with a man who *bluffed*? I can't believe it of you." Benedetti leaned over the chair. "No, we have evidence, and it is the evidence of your own mouth, sir.

"I will tell you what happened Friday night. Of course, you could come and go as you pleased. You grew up in those houses, on this estate. You, better than anyone, could slip through the woods quickly and quietly, and in and out of Alpha and Omega house without being seen. And who would there be for you to answer to? You are a grown man, older, as you frequently point out, than you appear. Furthermore, of course, you have the creamery on the grounds. There, at least, you are the unquestioned boss. No one there would question your comings or goings.

"So late Friday afternoon, you slipped away from the creamery, planted the kidnapping announcement in the estate mailbox, and sent the Federal Express ransom note to the factory for Swantek to read. You knew Mr. Jackson's routine; you knew the express company's and Swantek's. You could be assured the notes would be delivered in the proper order. Before you left the estate, or after your return, you slaughtered a cat you procured for the purpose, and left it as close to your uncle's cattery as you dared, hoping he'd find it and precipitate a 'crisis.'

"Luck was with you. Everything worked as you had anticipated. Your uncle stormed into Omega House cursing your father and blaming him for the death of the cat. Perhaps then, but probably earlier, you had told your uncle that you had formed the desire to adopt a kitten, but, of course, it wouldn't do for his brother to know yet. Perhaps you promised to keep the cat at the factory; perhaps you said you were procuring it for a friend or employee."

Chip's eyes gleamed. On some sick level, Ron could see he was enjoying this. "Sure. Sandy, maybe. She was the cat type."

"Very likely," the Professor said. "In any case, you met your uncle, overpowered him, tied him, gagged him, and took him for a ride in his own car. As you did, you used a miniature portable tape recorder to describe your trip. You made the actual drive, so that the timing between your supposedly spontaneous messages would be right. You planted that first sign by the side of the road and left a few other traces of yourself at the sites you would pretend to be the following night.

"It must have been fun for you, with your uncle powerless beside you, to enact your charade, preparing your alibi for the time, some twenty-four hours later, when you would murder him. Was he conscious?"

Chip didn't answer.

"I rather think he was," Benedetti said. "The autopsy showed no blows to your uncle's head, and revealed no trace of drugs in his system. Having him conscious, confused, and frightened added sauce to the feast of evil you were preparing for yourself. But no matter. That is something else we can discuss when you are safely behind bars.

"Finally, having completed your zigzag course, and having provided yourself with enough time for the following evening, you drove the Lincoln Town Car to the barn. There you left your uncle tied to this chair.

"That was something we missed. The fact that Clyde Pembroke was hidden right on the family estate was more than just a gesture of contempt—it was a coldly calulated practical move. It obviated the need for another vehicle, one that might be traced. You could simply walk home through the woods.

"Everything was going your way. Your uncle was safely abducted and hidden. You might have killed this kitten, but I suppose it amused you to leave your uncle a Manx cat as a companion for his last day on earth. I suppose also that you transported the kitten in the trunk, since we heard nothing of it on the tape. The smooth ride of the heavy luxury car had ensured a high-quality, easily understandable tape for you to play for any benefit over the cellular phone on the following night."

Benedetti rubbed his chin. "And how it must have amused you when I, myself, played directly into your hands. You would report your movements on a cellular phone, I said, so that we might keep you safe. Here was the World-Famous Niccolo Benedetti advancing your own plan for you! Of course, had I failed to, you would have suggested it yourself. You said as much before your departure Saturday night."

"I was afraid for you, you bastard," Ron said. "I *liked* you."

Chip was still unruffled. "I'm a likable guy," he said. "I have my kinks, like anybody else, but I'm very likable."

"Don't," Ron said, "get me started on what you are, okay?"

"And so you took off," the Professor went on, "in the Samurai, a small, two-seated, four-wheel-drive vehicle with a canvas roof. You had a million dollars in the back, but as we have already said, that meant nothing to you. You left Omega House, with our concern for your welfare ringing in your ears. How hard it must have been not to laugh out loud at us."

"Actually, it's pretty difficult right now," Chip said. "If I weren't so furious, I'd be amused. Or vice versa."

Benedetti ignored him.

"And so you drove off. Before you were even off the property, you activated the tape—you had a miniature tape player concealed either in the car or on your person. You had carefully prepared us for not being able to speak to you. You played the tape, probably through a relay direct to the mouthpiece of the telephone and not through the air—a simple matter to construct, or even to buy. An earphone plug at one end of a wire, and two alligator clips at the other.

"You followed the routine of the previous night for a time, then you went to the barn, and with this cat"—he elevated Nimrod in his arms—"for a witness, you coldly strangled your uncle to death, far enough in advance so that the medical examiner's report would show that he died at a time we would be sure *you* were on the road, still following the senseless instructions of the kidnappers. Of all the people in the world, you were the one who could not *possibly* have killed your uncle. You alone had a perfect alibi.

"Except," the Professor said. "Except for one thing. Your tape. That smooth-voiced, high-fidelity tape. It was recorded in a luxury car, a vehicle designed to minimize external noise. That night, *you* were riding in a vehicle that may have many virtues, but quiet and smooth-riding are not among them.

"If you had truly been talking to us from the Samurai, we would have heard engine noise. We did not. We would have heard the sound of other cars going by you, as they inevitably would, even on the quiet back roads you so deliberately chose. And we would have heard *the unsteady, shaky voice of a man in a vehicle moving on the pitiful gravel roads of the estate*. We would have heard them at the very beginning and very end of your purported journey. We should—*I* should—have noticed the lack of this sooner. We have each been remarking on the roughness all week. But we did not hear that. Did we, Chip?"

Ron now knew what the Professor's last canvas showed—a shaky set of human vocal cords.

Chip was not quite as blithe as he'd been a little while ago, but he was by no means quivering. He ran his tongue along the inside of his mouth.

"Is that," he said, "all you've got?"

"For now," Ron told him. "It'll do for Viretsky to haul you in. Then he'll go around with pictures of you. The electronic stuff you used came from somewhere—he'll find out where you bought it. It went somewhere, too. I can see two hundred state troopers with dogs, combing the estate. There's the stuff that went into the bomb you blasted Sandy with. The evidence will pile up, Chip. You'll be buried under it."

Humbert Pembroke II raised his eyebrows. Then he started to laugh. "Well, maybe I will. Possibly. You might find that stuff. Maybe. So what?"

"I don't think you'll like it in jail, Chip. I really don't."

"I won't go to jail. Are you kidding? Two or three nights in the Viretsky Hilton, maybe, but that's it. I've got a couple of hundred million dollars behind me, Ron. When I give my poor, ailing pop my sob story, I'll have all the lawyers that money can buy—and the best ones, too. And I'll have a bunch of oh-so-respectful expert witnesses, a parade of them, telling why my rotten childhood drove me crazy, you know? I mean, I was raised by a servant who wasn't even a goddam *nanny*. What the hell, a guy who'd use a chemical to drive birds away from his father's woods, a guy who'd bash cats (except for your 'witness' over there; I kind of like *him*), must be *nuts*, don't you think? Well, a jury will think so. And the Pembroke fortune, augmented by the smoke scrubber, I might add, will pay for appeal after appeal until a jury *says* so." Chip smiled amiably.

"So, let's chalk this up to a pleasantly wasted afternoon, shall we? Or does the World-Famous Professor Benedetti want to spend the rest of his life in Harville, testifying against a poor, sick boy?"

"Neither," Benedetti said. He nodded to Ron.

Ron grabbed Chip's arm and hauled him out of his seat. "This is called a citizen's arrest. I'm arresting you. Viretsky can word the exact charge."

Chip shrugged. His expression did not change. "It's your funeral."

"We'll see. Oh, there's something else you ought to know. *Janet!*" Ron yelled. "Bring them in now."

The door of the big, old barn had not been shut all the way. Now it opened wide, and Janet stepped in, flanked by two old men, one white, one black.

"Were you gentlemen able to hear everything?" Benedetti asked.

"Loud and clear, Professor," Janet replied.

"*Va bene*," the Professor said.

Ron said, "Let's go."

Chip's face was stunned. He let Ron lead him along like a zombie. Near the door, however, he stopped. "Dad . . . ," he said, but he was unable to say more.

That was the last word spoken, though there were sounds of sobbing.

Tears ran freely down the brown cheeks of Lewis Jackson.

Henry Pembroke's face was stone.

T h i r t e e n

Benedetti was watching *Once Upon a Time in the West* up in his sitting room when Ron knocked and entered. It was one of the old man's favorite movies. Nimrod, now eight months old, squirted into the room ahead of Ron, and immediately attacked the old man's shoes.

Benedetti laughed and grabbed the mighty hunter by the scruff of the neck, then proceeded to stroke him. A low purr came from somewhere under the red fur.

"Yes, *amico*? To what do I owe the pleasure of your visit?"

"I got a phone call from Viretsky down in Harville. He thought we'd like to know. Henry Pembroke died this afternoon."

Benedetti gave a somber nod. "I don't suppose his son will care one way or the other."

"No. The state attorney has already taken steps to make sure Chip doesn't get out of the joint to go to the funeral."

"Sound."

"Viretsky wants to know if we'll be going. Says Jackson would like us there."

"What did you tell him?"

"I said I'd call him back."

The old man continued to stroke the purring kitten. "What do you think?"

"I think, unfortunately, that we'd better go. We owe the poor bastard that much."

"We could not have let him maintain his illusion of his son, *amico*. Not at the cost of letting such an evil one go free."

"I know, I know. I did my part, didn't I?"

232 • William L. DeAndrea

"Indeed you did. Still, it's not one of the investigations we
will look back on fondly, is it? I make such a point of studying humility because its own lessons are so harsh. But, tell
me, how is Chief Viretsky?"

"Oh, he's great. Pennsylvania Law Officer of the Year, and
he's grateful. Hinted we might be getting invited to a wedding soon."

"Miss Ackerman?"

"Yeah. Flo's quit the EPA, you know. She's working for
Pembroke Industries, now. Selling smoke scrubbers. So we
can all breathe easier."

"I detest puns."

"No, I think that's their real slogan. Oh . . . and Viretsky's
had a sneak peek at Henry's will, apparently. Henry's money
and stock in the company all go to a foundation for AIDS research."

"A worthy cause."

"But Swantek is the trustee. He's running the whole business, for as long as he wants. Complete control. Hope he's up
to it."

"People rise to occasions, Ronald."

"Or sink to them."

There was a long silence. Then Ron said, *Maestro?* It
scares me."

"What does?"

"Chip Pembroke. Oh, his father left him a bottle of grape
soda in the will, by the way."

Benedetti laughed. "Why should he scare you? There is no
danger of his being released to seek revenge."

"It's not that, it's— *Maestro,* there's no such thing as an
evil baby."

"No."

"Well, with Janet due any day, I just wonder—how does a

Chip Pembroke *get* that way? All the *hatred* he had for every-body close to him, to want to hurt them so much . . ."

"If I could answer that, *amico*, my work would be finished, and I could retire. But I will say this—Chip Pembroke could not have hated others so much if he didn't hate himself the most."

"I'm going to be a father sometime in the next two weeks. The amnio told us it's going to be a boy." Ron thought it over. "Well, I can't guarantee he's going to love himself, but I can make sure he never doubts for a moment that Janet and I love him."

"And each other."

"And each other," Ron echoed.

"That is wisdom, my friend. The rest is up to God."

"Thanks, *Maestro*."

"The advice of an old bachelor on fatherhood cannot be worth much."

"I appreciate it, anyway." Ron got up and headed for the door.

"Oh, and Ronald?" the old man said.

"Yes?"

"Will you please take your infernal cat with you so I may watch my movie in peace?"

Laughing, Ron went over and picked up the cat. "Come on, Nimrod," he said. "I'll practice on you for a while. If I can love a shoe-killer like you, a baby has nothing to worry about."